What would she be like in bed?

It was some time since he'd had a woman, and something told him Opal Clemenger would be all woman. And he wanted her. And he would have her.

"Maybe there's a chance I will accept your conditions," he said.

"You will?"

"But only on one proviso," he added. "Quite simply, you only have to agree to do one thing."

"And…and what would that be?"

He looked her squarely in the eyes. "Marry me, Opal Clemenger. I will invest in your hotel chain, on your terms, if you will agree to become my wife."

BRIDES OF CONVENIENCE

Forced into marriage—by a millionaire!

Four women demanded for marriage…
by four very sexy men who get everything
they want. And what they want is their new
wives in the bedroom.

Read all four wedding stories in this
new collection by your favorite authors,
available in Promotional Presents May 2007:

The Lawyer's Contract Marriage—
Amanda Browning

A Convenient Wife—
Sara Wood

The Italian's Virgin Bride—
Trish Morey

The Mediterranean Husband—
Catherine Spencer

THE ITALIAN'S
VIRGIN BRIDE
TRISH MOREY

BRIDES OF CONVENIENCE

TORONTO • NEW YORK • LONDON
AMSTERDAM • PARIS • SYDNEY • HAMBURG
STOCKHOLM • ATHENS • TOKYO • MILAN • MADRID
PRAGUE • WARSAW • BUDAPEST • AUCKLAND

ISBN-13: 978-0-373-82051-1
ISBN-10: 0-373-82051-8

THE ITALIAN'S VIRGIN BRIDE

First North American Publication 2007.

This edition published by arrangement with Harlequin Books S.A.

® and TM are trademarks of the publisher. Trademarks indicated with ® are registered in the United States Patent and Trademark Office, the Canadian Trade Marks Office and in other countries.

www.eHarlequin.com

Printed in U.S.A.

THE ITALIAN'S
VIRGIN BRIDE

To Mum and Dad because, obviously, you guys have so much to answer for☺

Almost fifty years together—
that takes a certain kind of resilience,
if not a special brand of love.

Thanks for everything.

CHAPTER ONE

DOMENIC SILVAGNI was only one third through the report when the intercom buzzed for the second time in five minutes. He growled in irritation and slammed his fountain pen down so fast it skidded right across the leather-bound blotter.

His father again.

No one else could have made it past the snarling Ms Hancock, the human Rottweiler he'd been assigned as his PA during his visit to the Silvers hotel chain's premier Sydney hotel, and who ran interference for him with ruthless efficiency. Which was exactly what he needed if he was ever to analyse this report. Somewhere amidst this mountain of facts and figures and market research lay the solution to the hotel chain's flagging fortunes in Australia. And he was determined to discover whatever it was in time to make his flight to Rome tonight.

So much for demanding 'no calls'. Trust his father to pull rank on him. And he wasn't in the mood for another lecture. Not if it concerned *those* photos again—the two photos published in the gossip rag *Caught In The Act*. He considered his personal life his own business but that magazine had just made it everybody's.

And Guglielmo Silvagni knew damned well the

playboy image the rag bestowed upon his son was a pure fabrication, but he was still less than happy about it.

'You can do better than supermodels and starlets,' he'd asserted. 'Find someone with some intelligence, some spunk—someone to give you a run for your money.'

Emma and Kristin might justifiably have been offended had they heard his father's assessment of them. After all, even rising Hollywood starlets and supermodels couldn't make it on looks alone, though they had those in abundance.

Not to mention jealousy. Both had taken it pretty personally when the photos were published.

Without doubt the whole episode had been an inconvenience. But that didn't mean he'd be better off settling down, as his father kept suggesting. He wasn't looking for a wife. He wasn't looking for a family. No matter how many times his father lectured him he was leaving it too late.

Too late! Hell, he was only thirty-two. Hardly over the hill.

The light on the intercom button kept flashing at him accusingly. *Liar*, it seemed to say. He groaned in frustration—*now he was starting to think like his father*—and lifted the handset.

'Tell my father I'll call him back later. After I've got through this report.'

'I'm sorry, Mr Silvagni, it's…actually not your father…'

He cocked an ear. Something was wrong. She'd

lost her usual 'take-no-prisoners' tone. And for the first time since he'd arrived, he'd even say the snapping Ms Hancock sounded flustered.

'There's this woman...' she continued.

He gritted his teeth. *A pity his Rottweiler had lost hers.*

He could understand Guglielmo Silvagni getting past this line of last defence. He *was* Silvers Hotels. Together with his own father, Domenic's late grandfather, he had developed it from a three-room operation in Naples into a worldwide five-star success. And even though his father had retired to the rural countryside of Tuscany after a lengthy battle with cancer, and it was Domenic who now headed up the international operation, his father still wielded power. *But a woman?*

'I told you, *absolutely* no calls.'

'She's not on the phone,' she squeezed out on a breath, before he had a chance to terminate the conversation. 'She's here. She said it's urgent, that you'd want to see her.'

Domenic leaned back in his leather executive chair, drumming his fingers on the edge of the broad desk. 'Who is it?' he asked, while his brain did a quick scan of the known whereabouts of his latest companions. Last thing he heard Emma was on location in Texas shooting her latest film, while Kristin was doing a photo shoot for *Vogue* in Morocco. And neither of them was speaking to him after that damned photo fiasco, so neither even knew he'd made this last-minute trip to Australia.

'Her name is Opal Clemenger. From Clemengers. It's a family-owned chain of three prestige boutique hotels. There's one just down at the Rocks—'

'I know all about Clemengers,' he snapped. 'What does she want?'

'She said she has a deal for you. An opportunity too good to refuse. Should I send her in?'

Opal held her breath as she stood next to the PA's desk, white-knuckled fingers clutching the file of material she'd hastily assembled in preparation, hoping above hope that he would agree to this last-minute meeting.

Surely his interest was piqued? Surely he would be asking himself why the owner of the only six-star boutique hotel in Sydney would be dropping by at late notice? Surely he wouldn't think it was a social call?

And he *had* to agree to see her. The future of Clemengers and its staff depended on it.

'Tell her to make an appointment,' the voice over the intercom snapped back. 'I'll be back in two weeks. Oh, and I'll work through lunch. Can you send in some coffee and something to eat?'

The receptionist confirmed the order and then looked up at Opal apologetically as her master's voice disappeared with a final crackle of static. 'I'm sorry, dear. It's so unusual for me to interrupt him; I really thought he'd be curious to see you. I'm afraid you'll have to come back. Can you do that?'

Opal shook her head, teeth raking her bottom lip.

Two weeks was far too late. She had two days to
stitch up this deal. Just two days to find someone to
invest in Clemengers, someone who would understand and continue the business as a going concern.
Someone totally unlike McQuade, a corporate vulture
just out to pick up bargain real estate in prime locations so that he could knock the buildings down and
put up yet more overpriced blocks of flats.

In just over a day tenders would close, and unless
she found a white knight to come to the rescue of
Clemengers, McQuade was front-runner to win the
tender, her family would lose everything they'd
worked for and at least two hundred loyal staff would
lose their jobs.

*And there was no way she'd let the hotel go to
McQuade.*

'I have to see him today,' she said. 'I have no
choice.' She turned away, moving automatically over
the plush rose-coloured carpet and searching for solutions but finding none amongst the gentle pastel art-
work adorning the walls, only half aware of Ms
Hancock in the background speaking to Room
Service.

Maybe she'd missed something. She flipped open
the folio she still held, pausing over the collection of
magazine and newspaper clippings and internet arti-
cles she'd put together as soon as she'd heard of
Domenic's visit to his southern-hemisphere interests.
Maybe hidden amongst all these papers was the key
she needed?

The pages slid apart at a glossy magazine page.

There, under the heading 'Five-Star Playboy', were two photographs of Domenic, each photo featuring him with a different woman. Very blonde, very young women. If they were the kind of women Domenic Silvagni was interested in, then it was little wonder he'd fail to appreciate the buttoned-up talent sitting outside his office.

Her focus moved to the man each of them looked up at adoringly. Five-star playboy, indeed. The title fitted him just as perfectly as the tailored dinner suit of one photo, the silky black shirt of the other. He wore the doe-eyed women clinging to his arm like accessories.

Little wonder he could get away with it. Domenic Silvagni was one good-looking man. He stared out at her from the pictures, dark, sultry eyes outlined with the sort of thick lashes any woman in her right mind would kill for. His fringe, slightly longer than the rest of his short layered hair, was flicked to one side. Strong lips tweaked as if hinting at a secret, framed with a lean square jaw that spoke of power and influence.

Even without his money Domenic Silvagni would be a catch. With his money, well, there was no doubt a queue of willing hopefuls.

And good luck to them, she thought bitterly. You deserved whatever you got marrying a playboy. Her mother's experience had taught her that much.

But whatever personal failings he had, she needed him. Or at least, she needed his money. And she needed it now.

Suddenly she wheeled around. 'I'll wait, if you don't mind. He has to come out eventually.'

Ms Hancock's eyes narrowed as her wrinkled lips formed a tight pucker. She looked from side to side, as if checking if anyone was in earshot. But there was no one to be seen along the wide corridor of carpet that led from the bank of brass-framed lifts to the outer office. There were no guest rooms on this fortieth floor, no visitors coming and going, no laundry hampers rolling along to interrupt proceedings.

Still, she leaned forward in her chair, and whispered conspiratorially, 'I need to step out for five minutes, and Room Service will be bringing lunch up at any time. You wouldn't go do anything silly, now, would you?'

Opal felt a genuine smile return to her lips. The first real smile she'd had since learning of the dire circumstances facing Clemengers three months ago. And that smile was directed right at Deirdre Hancock, former secretary to her father some twenty years ago.

She'd known it was a good omen as soon as she'd walked into the ante-office and recognised Deirdre sitting there. And Deirdre had jumped up immediately and thrown her arms around Opal for a mighty hug as if she hadn't changed a bit, even though she'd long ago traded her six-year-old braids for a sleek shoulder-length style.

Whatever Deirdre was now doing at Silvers, Opal had no idea, but working for Domenic Silvagni was obviously no picnic. The man was downright rude from the exchange she'd heard, while Deirdre was a treasure. Sure, she might look like a dragon, in her severe navy suit and sensible court shoes, but from what she remembered her father saying, Deirdre had never been anything less than organised, efficient and polite. And she was doing her best to get her in to see him. Domenic didn't deserve her.

She winked back. 'Not a chance,' she said.

Five minutes later, Deirdre bundled a bunch of papers together and Opal sensed the imminent arrival of the lunch trolley. Adrenaline kicked into her veins at the same time as the sudden realisation of what the PA was actually risking. 'Look, Deirdre, I don't want you to lose your job over this.'

Ms Hancock sniffed. 'Who knows, dear?' She leaned her tiny frame closer and squeezed her arm. 'He might even thank me for it. Besides which, I'm retiring next week. What's he going to do—sack me? Now, I've switched the phone through to the copy room, where I'll be, so you won't be interrupted.' Opal barely had time to murmur her thanks before she was gone.

Less than a minute later Room Service rolled the silver-domed trolley alongside Ms Hancock's desk. The fresh-faced young man looked around, his gaze finally settling on Opal. 'Ms Hancock's order,' he half said, half asked.

'She'll be right back.'

He nodded and, apparently satisfied, headed back to the service lift, disappearing in a hum of lift motors and cushioned doors.

She took one more rapid-fire breath and pushed herself off her chair. *This was it!*

CHAPTER TWO

'WHO are you?'

Opal made it no more than three paces into the expansive office before the man sitting behind the broad mahogany desk glanced up.

'And where's Ms Hancock?'

For a second Opal's feet wouldn't move. But she had to get more than a metre inside the door. She couldn't make her case from here. Barely looking up, in case his face was darker than his words, she plastered on a bright smile totally at odds with her churning insides and pressed on, wheeling the trolley closer to the desk. 'I've brought your lunch.'

Studiously avoiding his gaze, she was aware of his body swinging up in his seat and his elbows colliding with the table. 'I can see that,' he growled. 'But how did you get in here?'

Opal busied herself with the trolley. She lifted the silver lid from one salver—pasta with artichokes and bacon. The other revealed veal escalopes with asparagus in a brandy cream sauce. 'I think the pasta first,' she said, transferring the first dish to a vacant spot on his desk.

He ignored her and strode to the door, flinging it open. 'Ms Hancock!' he shouted. 'Ms Hancock!'

'I think you'll find she's in the copy room. I didn't want your lunch to get cold in the meantime.'

He turned then. Without looking up, Opal felt it like a blast from a furnace. 'Who the hell are you?'

Fortified with a deep gulp of air, she finally lifted her eyes to face him and straight away wished she hadn't. It was Domenic all right. Those dark eyes, the strong jaw. She should have been ready. And yet— the picture torn from a magazine was just a mere facsimile of the man who stood before her. Nothing in those photos revealed the power, the sheer presence of the man, the masculine physicality he projected.

The heat!

Under her silk suit her skin prickled and firmed. She swallowed involuntarily, tasted fear and kicked up her chin in defiance. She had a job to do. And he was just a man, after all. A playboy to boot—*the very worst kind of man.*

She battled to remind herself of that as she searched for the words that should have fallen off her tongue much more easily.

'Opal Clemenger.' She gave a wry smile. 'Thank you for finding the time to see me. I appreciate you're very busy.'

He snorted and pulled the door open wide.

'I'm not finding the time to see you. I said you could come back in two weeks. Better still, not at all.' He gestured to the open door with his free hand. 'Now, if you'll excuse me, I have work to do.'

'But I haven't had a chance to tell you my proposal yet.'

'Does it occur to you, Ms Clemenger, that may be because I'm not interested?'

She made no move towards the door and she could feel the anger rising in the man facing her. 'Your pasta is getting cold.'

'Then the sooner you remove yourself, the sooner I can eat.'

'We can talk while you have lunch.'

'I was going to work while I had lunch.'

'That's not healthy.'

'Arguing with women who don't know when they've outstayed their welcome is not healthy. Leave. *Now.*'

'Not until you hear what I have to offer.'

'Or do I have to make you?' His head tilted, and his lips curled, as if he was speculating on whether he'd have to, and her fear cranked up a notch. If he so much as touched her...

'I have an opportunity for you,' the words spilt out, before she could think too far along that disturbing path, 'a chance to give the Silvers hotel chain the edge it's looking for—the edge it needs.'

'I see I'm going to have to make you.' He moved away from the door, each step bringing him closer. Instinctively she felt herself draw back. She hadn't been prepared for his height, nor for his sheer animal power. Right at that moment she felt more like an animal of prey than the owner and CEO of Australia's most prestigious boutique hotel chain, with Domenic the hunter, drawing ever closer, ever more threatening.

She knew she was speaking fast. But she had to get through to him. Had to make an impression. Before the opportunity was lost to her forever.

'Something to lift Silvers beyond this five-star mediocrity…'

He stopped, not two paces from her, and scoffed. 'Five-star *what*?'

She seemed to grow a good inch taller, though his six-foot-two frame still cleared hers by six inches or so, and fire flickered in the depths of her blue-green eyes. The corners of her mouth tweaked up in such a way that told him she thought she'd just scored some kind of point.

She had a nerve, this woman. Somehow managing to get past his assistant, forcing her way into his office and accusing his business of *mediocrity*. Nerve, or stupidity. Either way, she was leaving.

'Mediocrity, Mr Silvagni. Five-star used to mean something special. Now it just means more of the same. People don't want that. People want an experience. People want to feel *special*.'

'Thank you, Ms Clemenger, for your astute observations. But if I need to have my business analysed, I'm sure I can find more qualified people than you to do it.'

'Is that so? Then if it's so easy, why are you in Sydney at all? You'd have the resources for an army of analysts to devise the kind of strategies Silvers needs. Surely you've got better things to do with your time?'

He bristled, recognising the attempt he'd made to

undermine her position had backfired. She'd made it backfire. Ms Clemenger was really starting to get his back up, yet for all that he was curious. Silvers did have a problem. Would it hurt to hear her out? He crossed his arms and rested one hip on the side of the desk.

'You've got five minutes,' he said. 'Start talking.'

For a few seconds she seemed at a loss for words and for that he was grateful. For once he didn't have to concentrate on her words, and he had a chance to focus on the forthright Ms Clemenger herself.

She wasn't half the challenge to look at as she was to listen to. Brown hair. No, not quite brown. More like the colour of warm syrup. Full, lush mouth. Clear, almost translucent skin, with eyes that knew both intelligence and emotion. He'd noticed the way they'd widened when she'd finally raised her eyes to meet his, the flare of recognition and something else—shock or fear? But if she'd been scared, still she hadn't backed off. *He liked that.*

His appraisal moved down.

Her cobalt-blue suit fitted her well enough, yet hinted at curves not quite revealed, and maybe, just maybe, if she sat down in the chair behind her that skirt might just ride up enough for him to tell if the rest of her long legs were as shapely as those calves suggested.

She remained standing.

'Mr Silvagni.'

He dragged his attention back from speculation about her legs to her mouth—and those lips.

'Domenic, please.'

She looked at him and for a moment he thought she was going to fight about even that. Then she nodded slightly.

'Domenic,' she said softly, as if testing. He liked the way she said his name. Her voice was warm and mellow and somehow her slight yet unmistakable Australian accent helped to smooth the rhythm of the syllables. She had the kind of voice you wouldn't mind waking up to—now the desperation factor had gone from it.

'Like other major hotel chains in Australia and, indeed, even worldwide, the Silvers chain is suffering from a downturn in occupancy rates. There just isn't the volume of travellers to fill the hotels. The pie has shrunk and the pieces are smaller. Marketing might increase one chain's share over another, but it's a short-term gain and can be easily lost in the next round of media advertising.'

He shifted, unfolded his arms and dropped his hands to his thighs. Nothing she said was new. He'd been reading the same bleak news in the report that was still sitting atop his desk.

'And assuming that your assessment is right, I take it you have a solution to this problem?' If she thought he sounded doubtful, she was right.

She clutched her hands together and he noticed her long fingers and clear buffed nails. No rings.

'I have an opportunity for Silvers Hotels, if you're astute enough to appreciate it.'

'I see,' he said, ignoring the none-too-subtle rebuke. 'And that "opportunity" is?'

She took a deep breath. There was no way he couldn't notice, with her chest at his eye level. She had shape, under that suit. More than a hint now. There were breasts and hips and a cinched-in waist. He shifted his gaze upwards and was immediately rewarded by a distinct flush to her cheeks. *How about that? The lady was shy.*

He cocked an eyebrow, questioning.

'Clemengers owns three six-plus-star boutique hotels, located on prime sites in each of Sydney, Melbourne and Brisbane, and was founded by my late father over fifty years ago. Many of our staff have been with us for over twenty years, some more like forty. We're a family company that never outgrew its roots, its original mission statement—to be the best, to give the best, to the best.

'This downturn,' she continued, 'has affected us of course, but not to the same extent as it has Silvers. You have to ask yourself why.'

Domenic didn't want to ask, not her, but he wanted to know. He hadn't read anything about this in that report and one of the questions he was going to ask his finance manager once he got hold of him was why he had to learn this from the opposition, when he'd expected a comprehensive report.

'You don't want to know why?' she asked.

'I'm still listening,' he conceded with a nod. 'You tell me what you think.'

'I *know*,' she emphasised, 'Clemengers offers more

than just a place to stay. Clemengers offers an experience.'

'You're trying to say that Silvers doesn't offer an experience? We're one of the biggest hotel chains in the world. We would never have got there if we didn't offer the best.'

'But you don't offer a point of difference. You offer a fine product, a quality five-star product, but it's not the same thing. Just look at your clientele, for example—'

'What's wrong with it?' he interjected. 'Mick Jagger stayed in Silvers hotels during his last tour.'

'Exactly,' she continued. 'You have rock stars, businessmen, and tourists who like comfort. Clemengers, on the other hand, has prime ministers, sheikhs and those who appreciate luxury.'

He pushed off from the desk, strode three paces across the room and turned around. 'So what are you offering, then?'

'Simply the chance to share in the most prestigious hotel market in Australia. The chance to benefit and learn from our methods, so that you might strengthen the rest of your business. I'm offering a share of Clemengers.'

It was a crazy proposal and certainly there was nothing at all like it mooted in the report he'd been wading through this morning. And yet maybe it was just the sort of strategy Silvers should be looking at. Maybe that was what was lacking in that report. It was so much 'same old, same old'. Maybe it was about time someone thought outside the box.

'So what's in it for Clemengers? I can't believe you're doing this out of the goodness of your heart, to strengthen your own competition.'

She crossed to the window, gazing out across the vista of harbour bridge and opera house, ferry traffic and sails on a harbour that sparkled and shimmered in the early-afternoon sun, though he suspected she saw none of it.

'You could say,' she said, still facing the window, 'that Clemengers has a small cash-flow problem. My father took some bad advice that got him into trouble with the taxation department. I had no idea until after he died that we even had a problem. Six months ago I discovered how big that problem was. The banks were prepared to help—for a while.' She shook her head. 'We were making headway, until the latest tax office penalty notices came in. Now the banks won't extend.'

'How much is involved?'

She looked over and rattled off a figure that had him raising his eyebrows. 'That's exactly why the lawyers advised that Clemengers be sold. If the banks weren't interested—where else could we go? And yet the business is profitable—I can show you the figures to back that up. It's just that the outstanding back tax and penalties have to be paid, and soon.'

She sighed and gave a wan smile. Right now she looked tired. Tired and so vulnerable, not at all the intrepid, risk-taking female who'd pushed her way into his office demanding he listen to her proposal. Her head tilted to one side as she looked up at him.

'Clemengers has quietly been on the market for two months—why hasn't Silvers expressed any interest? For a business looking for solutions to its own problems, I would have thought someone might have made an expression of interest, or at least made some enquiries.'

Domenic didn't know. His Australian finance director had never passed on the information that the boutique hotel business was for sale. And while he may have had good reason to have discounted any opportunities the Clemenger deal might offer, why was there not even a mention of it in the report?

There was one way to find out. 'I think I've heard just about enough.' He moved to the desk, picked up the phone and dialled the finance director's number. She watched him from where she still stood, near the window, eyes wide, lips slightly parted, as if she'd been on the verge of saying something, copper flecks in her hair suddenly brought to life. Did she realise how beautiful she looked right now? Was that why she'd chosen that particular spot to stand, with the sunlight washing over her in a golden sheen?

Probably not, he decided while the phone rang at the other end, she seemed to lack the guile of the women he usually associated with.

Evan Hooper answered on the third ring and Domenic dragged his eyes from Opal and focused on the wall, where those peculiar eyes—not quite blue, not quite green—couldn't distract him. 'Evan, what can you tell me about the Clemengers sale?'

Opal drew in a deep breath. For a moment, just a

moment, she'd thought he was going to call Security and have her thrown out. Instead, she was still in with a chance. And he just had to see the benefits—there was far too much at stake for him not to.

'And the finances?' Domenic's terse questions to the finance director were meeting with very long answers.

'Then why?' His voice kicked up a few decibels before, on a muttered curse, he flung the phone down. For a second he stayed where he was, leaning his weight with his hands on the desk, his chest heaving, until he looked up at her and pushed himself upright. He swiped up his jacket.

'Come on, then, Ms Clemenger. Or may I call you Opal?'

'Of course, but—where are we going?'

'Where do you think? You're going to show me that six-plus-star hotel you're so proud of.'

She motioned to the desk, the plates of food still untouched. 'Your lunch…' she said.

'Leave it,' he said, putting a hand under her arm and guiding her towards the door. His face turned to hers and she caught his scent—woody tones over a mantle of male. It suited him. His teeth flashed as his mouth paused to smile. 'I want to see what you've got to offer.'

His touch was warm through her jacket, yet that still didn't stop the shiver that coursed through her. He meant the hotel, of course. Why would she imagine for a minute that she'd seen something else in the dark, heady gaze he'd turned her way? Sure he might be a playboy, but he was hardly likely to come the playboy with her—she wasn't the type, which was *exactly* the way she wanted it.

All she wanted from Domenic Silvagni was an investment, funds to ensure the future of Clemengers and its staff. If it took a playboy to save it, then so be it. Right now she couldn't afford to be too choosy.

Deirdre Hancock was back at her desk when they left the office. If she was surprised or pleased to see them together, she was the consummate professional again and didn't show it.

'I'll be out for the next couple of hours,' he said as he surged by. 'Would you arrange a car to pick us up downstairs?'

'Certainly, Mr Silvagni. By the way, your father rang again. I told him you were in conference.'

He stopped dead in his tracks, allowing Opal the opportunity to slip from his arm and retrieve her folio from the chair where she'd left it earlier.

'Did he leave a message?'

'He wonders if you're free Thursday evening in Rome. He and your mother have met a charming young woman they'd like to introduce you to.'

A noise like a deep snarl emanated from his throat.

'Do you have a message for him?' Deirdre asked.

'No. I'll deal with it later.' Then he turned to Opal and held out his hand towards the lift and she fell into step alongside him. She glanced back over her shoulder and caught an uncharacteristic thumbs-up Deirdre sent her way. *Thank you,* she mouthed back.

He followed her into the lift, his size dwarfing hers

in the reflection from the highly polished mirrors lining the interior. She turned to face the door, expecting Domenic to do the same, but he continued to face the back of the lift—and her—as the car hummed downwards. Her eyes sought anywhere to look but at him, and they sought refuge by studying the recession of numbers, which was altogether too slow for her liking.

But even avoiding his face, there was no escaping the raw heat of his proximity, the frank assessment of his gaze. Her body could feel it and responded, her skin tingling, her breasts firming, even as her eyes attempted to deny it. Even his scent, masculine and woody, seemed to taunt her. *Try to ignore me,* it mocked.

There was no ignoring him. But she could still show how unimpressed she was. Another time maybe she might have been intrigued, might have been attracted by the intense magnetism this man projected.

Another time and another man. But not now, not with Domenic Silvagni. *Never with a playboy.*

'How old are you?' he finally asked.

Her eyes snapped back to his. So that was what all the close inspection had been about. He'd been studying her for age lines. Given the adolescents he was used to dating, he was no doubt none too familiar with those.

'Is that relevant?'

'Twenty-four? Twenty-five?'

She straightened her spine, kicked up her chin. 'How old are you?'

'Thirty-two.'

'Oh.' Her indignation evaporated in the realisation she'd been churlish. He was only asking her age after all. It wasn't exactly privileged information. 'I was twenty-six in June.'

He arched one eyebrow high. 'And neither married nor engaged. Why is that?'

Self-consciously she covered one hand with the other, even though it was patently already too late.

'Maybe I have a boyfriend.'

'And do you? I wouldn't be surprised. You are a disarmingly beautiful woman.'

She felt the heat rise to her face and stared at the numbers—twenty-eight, twenty-seven—willing them to speed up before her cheeks were as red as the lights flashing their progress. 'Disarmingly beautiful'—what kind of a backhanded compliment was that? But there was no way she was going to ask.

Instead she said, 'I can't see what that has to do with the sale of Clemengers.'

He spun back against the wall of the lift, head raised to the ceiling. 'You're right. This isn't your problem.'

For a moment she was confused. Then realisation sank in. 'The phone call,' she said.

He nodded. 'The phone call. My father thinks I should be married. My mother makes it her career to interview every finishing-school graduate or European princess she comes across.'

Opal was reminded of the women photographed with Domenic. Clearly neither finishing-school graduates nor princesses. So what did he expect? His parents were no doubt concerned he'd end up hitched to one of those photo opportunists. In spite of herself, she felt a smile flirt around the corners of her mouth. 'I can see how that might be a problem—for someone like you.'

Her words snagged into him, their ragged edges scratching barbs across his consciousness. But if she expected that to put him on the defensive, she was very much mistaken. Notwithstanding his family connections, he hadn't got to where he was by rolling with the punches. That was something Ms Clemenger was going to have to learn.

He swung around and took a step closer, cramping her up against the back of the lift before dropping an arm each side of her to the brass handrail. She was trapped.

He saw the fright flicker in her widening eyes, the spark of alarm that glowed red in their greenish-blue depths, and was glad. 'Someone like me? That sounds very much like some kind of put-down, Ms Clemenger.'

But even as he waited for her response, something else happened in her eyes. The momentary flare cooled, a sheen of varnish turning them hard and cold and unreadable.

'Opal,' she said, only a touch shakily around the edges even though he could see the tightening white-knuckled grip on her folio, held up as a barrier between them. 'I said you could call me Opal.'

In spite of himself, he liked the way she said her

name. Liked the way her mouth opened and then pouted to form the 'p', widening once more until her pink tongue brushed her top teeth over the 'l'. There was something very sexy about the way her lips made that word. Come to think of it, there was something very sexy about her lips, period.

If only her eyes gave the same message.

'Opal,' he said, his lips curling but a few centimetres from hers. 'You wouldn't try to put down the man who was thinking about saving your business?'

This time her eyes met his savagely. 'And here was I thinking I was offering a solution for yours.'

He smiled. Those lips were so close he could just about reach over and sample them. 'That's not how it sounded to me.'

Now he had her nervous, her eyes darting from side to side, searching for escape almost as if she could read his mind. Her tongue flicked out, moistened her lips before darting back in.

'So maybe you weren't listening,' she said, her eyes fixed on the wall to his left.

'Oh, I've been listening,' he crooned, 'and watching, and wondering.'

Without Opal turning her head, her eyes found his before fleeing to fix on the wall once more.

'Wondering what?'

He dropped his head even closer. 'Whether that mouth tastes as good as it looks.'

He dipped his head, banishing the remaining few centimetres between them. His lips brushed hers, catching her sharp intake of air, and tasted warmth, life and just a hint of sweetness, before the lift doors behind him dinged, heralding their arrival at the ground floor and then opening with a whoosh.

'Excuse me,' she said, sounding a little bit breathless as she ducked her face, pushing past his arm and out to the freedom of the richly decorated marble foyer beyond. 'I think this is where I get off.'

He watched her shapely rear view as she fled for the safety of the foyer. She was some surprise package all right. He'd set out to intimidate her, not kiss her, but that didn't stop him thinking about the possibilities of a second chance.

'Lady,' he muttered under his breath as he followed her, 'this ride has only just begun.'

CHAPTER THREE

SHE was a fool. Opal poured herself a cup of Earl Grey tea from the silver pot, watching a flurry of tiny leaves swirl and tumble through the amber liquid. She didn't need to be a fortune-teller to know they were telling her the selfsame thing.

It was at least two hours since Domenic had pressed her against the back of the lift, had brushed her lips with his own and frozen her to the spot, and still she couldn't think about anything else.

He would be back to finish his coffee any moment, after excusing himself to take a private call on his mobile phone, and here she was, still thinking about what might have happened if those lift doors had not opened when they had, when she should be thinking about how to convince him to invest in the business.

By all accounts he had been impressed with the luxury and sheer class of Clemengers, from the moment Sebastian, the doorman, had greeted their entry with a formal nod to them both, his top hat and tails setting the tone for the tour to follow. He'd appreciated the generous size and furnishings of the suites, the bold antique tones that decorated each room, their sumptuous furnishings spelling wealth, luxury and prestige, with not a bland pastel water-colour print in sight.

He hadn't even balked when she'd shown him the figures, just studied them, nodding where he was clear, asking pertinent questions exactly where she'd expect anyone with the analytical ability to know when to drill down for further details.

Even the meal they'd just shared in The Pearl, Clemengers' award-winning restaurant, had been beyond reproach. Thai chilli king prawns, followed by the most tender fillet of steak, served on fried sweet-potato wedges and topped with lobster medallions in a white-wine sauce. Domenic had made a point of meeting the chefs before coffee, to compliment them personally and discuss their attitudes, their philosophies and their aspirations.

He would be doing none of this if he weren't seriously considering the idea of investing in Clemengers.

So it would be logical at this stage for her to be thinking about how she should close the deal. That would make sense. Close the deal and ensure Clemengers wasn't about to be gutted or razed and turned into so many more flats. Close the deal and ensure Clemengers could continue operating into the future. Close the deal...

Which didn't help explain one bit why she kept thinking about what had happened in the lift instead. Why was it so hard to forget about the gentle brush of his lips against hers, the heat of his breath next to her cheek, and the way his touch made her senses unfurl and open, like palm fronds given birth, stretching out into the humidity of a warm tropical morning?

He'd kissed her.

And she hadn't even attempted to stop him. From the moment she'd sensed his lips descending, she'd forgotten entirely why she was there. Even more damning, she'd forgotten what he was. He was a playboy. *The lowest kind of man.*

Sure he might end up investing in the hotel. For the sake of Clemengers, she'd have to look past the man's personal life. But she herself must never forget what he was. She should only think of her mother's sad and empty life to remind her what that would cost.

Absently she stirred a half-teaspoon of sugar into her tea. It was quiet in the restaurant. People spoke in hushed tones. The waiting staff were efficient and non-invasive, with no clatter or rattle of flatware and cutlery, and it was as if the traffic outside in the busy Rocks area didn't exist. But that didn't stop the prickle of awareness steadily creeping up her neck, then needling down her arms.

She was imagining it. All this thinking of the episode in the lift—she was not thinking rationally, and she was in danger of making a fool of herself. Obviously Domenic would have forgotten about it already. No doubt such incidents meant absolutely nothing to a man who had trouble committing to just one woman. She took a deep breath and focused on placing the spoon on the saucer, gently tinkling silver against porcelain.

She shivered, the creepy feeling persisting in spite of all her logical explanations. On pure impulse she looked across to her right and instantly her eyes snagged at the sight of him, Domenic, standing stock still and…and *watching her.*

For a second the space in the room evaporated in the arc between their eyes. Nothing happened, yet *something* happened between them in that infinitesimal moment that Opal could only wonder at. She felt hot, cold, shivering and flushed, all in the same amazing second his unreadable gaze washed over her. And then, just when she thought she couldn't look at him for a moment longer, he smiled and warmth filled her senses. Instinctively she knew the smile was for her and in spite of all her reservations, in spite of all the reasons why it shouldn't, the warmth inside her bloomed to a slow burn.

Annoyed at her burning cheeks, she battled to drag her eyes away as he moved between the tables towards her, slipping his mobile telephone into the top pocket of his fine cotton shirt as he did so.

'I'm sorry,' he said, resuming his seat. 'My father would not be denied any longer. I'm afraid that no matter how important any business, family must come first.'

'You don't need to apologise,' she said. 'The twins—my two sisters—and I are very close, although I don't see them now as often as I'd like.'

He took a sip of his long black and nodded approvingly. Even Clemengers' own special blend of coffee seemed to find favour with him. 'Tell me about them,' he said.

She put down her cup, thankful for the opportunity

to talk about her sisters, to think about someone else. 'Well, they're twenty-two. Sapphy—that's Sapphire— is the eldest by ten minutes. She's working in fashion design in Milan right now. She's making quite a name for herself by all accounts while she works with one of the big fashion houses. One day she wants to have her own label. And the way she's going, I believe she'll get it.

'Ruby lives in Broome while she gets first-hand knowledge of the pearl industry. Jewellery design is her first love. She's done some fabulous pieces.'

'And all of you are named after precious stones.'

She gave a small laugh. 'That was my mother's idea. She was the original Pearl. This restaurant,' she made a sweeping gesture with her hand, 'is named for her. She said we were all uniquely beautiful and inherently precious, and she wanted to give us names to reflect that.'

She paused, memories of her mother flooding back on a bitter-sweet tide. Her tender, sad-eyed mother, who had died alone when Opal was just nine, her spirit broken and her will to live erased. Her beautiful, gentle mother, whose only crime had been to love too much.

And everyone had thought she led the perfect life. A wealthy lifestyle, three beautiful little girls and even a plush restaurant named after her. No one else had seen the empty bed, the shame of her husband's constant infidelities and the broken-down shell of her marriage.

No one but Opal. Old enough to feel her mother's pain but far too young to be able to do anything about it, except swear that one day, some day, she would do something to help women who were trapped in marriages they couldn't escape.

'I approve of her philosophy.'

His words permeated her consciousness, dragging her from her reflections of her mother's wasted life.

'Do you?' She gave a brief laugh. 'I don't know if Dad would have though, if she'd given him a son. Somehow I can't imagine him tolerating a son called "Garnet".'

His lips pulled into a grimace. 'Perhaps not. How long ago did your father die?'

'Two years.' She frowned—that couldn't be right. 'No, more like two and a half now. A massive heart attack, apparently.'

'That's unfortunate,' he said. 'The stress of running hotels can be enormous, and I've found is often underrated by those outside the business.'

Opal looked out the window, feigning interest in the passing foot traffic, tourists visiting the various galleries and shops, red-faced businessmen returning to their offices after long liquid lunches.

Certainly people outside the industry had little or no idea of the stresses and strains of the business. Especially when coupled with the stresses and strains of trying to impress a nineteen-year-old pole dancer who was eager to prove herself very worthy of the position of the next Mrs Clemenger. Just maybe, if he'd spent more time stressing about their tax position, he would still be alive and the business wouldn't be in this mess now.

'And that left you in charge. Without even your sisters to help?'

It was her turn to shrug. There was no point in thinking about maybes. She couldn't change what had happened; though at times that knowledge didn't make the truth any easier to deal with. For if it hadn't been that particular girl his father had died in the arms of, it could have easily been any of a raft of others, lining up to be taken care of by a rich man old enough to be their grandfather. It was a miracle he'd never taken that final step of marrying one of them. Obviously he was a man who liked to pick and choose, and at least it had saved the business that complication.

'That's just the way things turn out. And both Sapphy and Ruby have such artistic flair—it would be unfair to make them work in the hotel business when they have a calling in another field. Whereas I've had a passion for Clemengers ever since I can remember, always wanting to help, always wanting to be involved. I can't imagine doing anything else.'

His eyebrows peaked. 'Which is where I come in, I take it. It would be understandably hard to let go.'

His words bristled. For want of something to do she pushed aside her now empty teacup and saucer.

'There's more to saving Clemengers than what I want. For a start, there are more than two hundred staff who depend on this hotel chain continuing to

operate for their own and for their families' livelihoods.

'And,' she continued, 'there's a tradition. No one
else provides the type and scale and class of accommodation as Clemengers. That has to be worth
saving.'

He held up a hand. 'And you say this McQuade is
likely to win the tender? How can you know that in
advance?'

Her lips tightened as she nodded, the name sticking
into her as effectively as a knife. 'I was due for an
appointment with the broker and I was just paying the
taxi driver when I overheard two office juniors dis-
cussing the bids over a cigarette outside the building.'

'But you're sure?'

'No doubt at all. I was so shocked I confronted the
broker and he eventually confirmed it. I can be pretty
persuasive when I want to be, you know.'

The corners of his mouth turned up and his eyes
gleamed. 'I had noticed something of the sort.'

She looked up at him sharply, not entirely certain
he wasn't laughing at her.

'So you need a bidder who will outbid McQuade.'

'Yes,' she said, recovering some composure. 'The
bids close tomorrow at five o'clock, so there's not
much time.'

'I see. And assuming I win the tender, I assume
control of Clemengers and its three hotels and everything that goes with it.'

'Well, sort of.' She licked her lips. 'I was thinking
maybe more of a share of the business.'

'What do you mean, a share of the business? If my offer is the highest, I win the business lock, stock and barrel.'

'In a way, but I thought that maybe if I continued to manage the operation, and run it as a separate entity within the Silvers hotel chain, then you might accept a smaller share.'

'How much of a smaller share?'

'I was thinking, maybe forty-nine per cent?'

'Now you are joking.' His voice went up a number of decibels. 'You expect me to outbid every other offer in the market, each of which is for ownership of Clemengers outright, I assume…' he took her silence as assent before continuing '…and yet I will own and control only forty-nine per cent. That is not a deal worth making. That is not a deal at all.'

'I assure you it's no joke. You get a large share of the business and you get continuity in management— good management. I will stay on, working with Clemengers and with Silvers Hotels, where required. And within a year you'll be reaping the rewards of a positive cash flow and you'll be able to use the techniques you find in Clemengers in Silvers' own operations. There have to be huge spin-offs for your other hotels. So even with less than complete ownership, you're still getting a great deal.'

It had to sound convincing. It was the only way she was going to be able to keep Pearl's Place—the refuge she'd established in a run-down inner-city terraced house four years ago—open for business.

Pearl's Place was her secret, something she'd done

because even though she'd never been able to help her own mother, other women would have a place to go, a place to flee. She'd bought the property with her own money and most of her own personal allowance went direct to the refuge, but without control of Clemengers there was no doubt what small funding it required would be one of the first sacrifices of the new merger. If she could retain fifty-one per cent of the business, however, her secret would be safe and funding would be ensured.

It was a far better scenario than if McQuade's offer succeeded. Then there would barely be enough to satisfy the demands of the taxation department and the banks. She'd be able to make some sort of contribution out of any remaining share of her own, but after that Pearl's Place would be on its own. She wouldn't let that happen.

He shook his head. 'No. This is not complete ownership. It is not even control of the business you are offering. It is a junior partner you want, but for the greatest investment. No one would accept a deal that one-sided, least of all a Silvagni.' His hand slammed down on the table so hard she flinched.

'There is no way I would ever accept less than fifty per cent on principle, especially where I have just paid over the odds for one hundred per cent. But if you really think your management skills are worth something, I will ensure you receive a suitable remuneration package. It will be worth your while continuing.'

'That's all you can offer? After I have brought you

this opportunity? Don't you see that you wouldn't even have had this chance if it weren't for this huge tax liability hanging over our heads?'

'That, as they say in the classics,' he said, with a look of complete satisfaction, 'is not my problem.'

'But you would have missed out on this opportunity entirely without my intervention. Your finance department hadn't even considered Clemengers' sale as worthy of your notice. Surely, if the deal is worth something, you should be prepared to acknowledge that fact.'

'And surely you realised that once the business was sold, you would lose control completely.'

'Yes, but that was before I spoke with you. I thought you understood this business, could see the benefits of a joint operation.'

'You forget, first and foremost, I am a businessman. I am not running a charitable institution.'

'I am not looking for charity!'

'Then why do you expect something from me that you have not asked from the other bidders?'

She couldn't tell him. Not the real reason. 'I just thought you were more attuned to the business, that you might understand. I now see I was wrong to expect you to look at it my way.'

'So my offer still stands. A higher bid than McQuade, you end up with an appropriate remuneration package, and Clemengers is saved from the bulldozers.'

She was silent for a few seconds and Domenic wondered what was going through her mind. Her eyes swirled with colour and he could practically see the machinations going on behind them. She couldn't be serious. Any normal person would be satisfied with saving her precious hotels from destruction. Well, she'd made her stand and he hoped she understood his. There was no way he'd accept anything less than one hundred per cent ownership. *No way.*

'I'll have to think about it,' she said at last, rising from the table as if he'd been dismissed.

He looked up sharply without saying a word. He didn't have to say a word—she should be able to tell he was furious. He'd just wasted hours and all for nothing. No one had ever turned down a deal like the one he was offering. No one would. No one in their right mind, that was.

He had to hand it to her. Here she was with a solid offer to save her business, by far the best offer she had on the table and the best offer she was going to get in the twenty-four hours she had left, and she wanted to think about it, as if the ball was in *her* court.

She was not like the people he usually dealt with; people who exchanged properties and investments and millions of dollars with hardly a blink, who knew when to take a good deal and when to break one. Who knew when they were asking too much.

Opal Clemenger didn't fit that mould. Opal Clemenger came with her own. He let his eyes wander over her woven-silk-clad figure, the rise and fall of her chest betrayed by the play of light over the textured fabric, the swell of her hips accentuated by the nipped-in waist of her jacket, and felt his eyebrows rise in appreciation as his anger turned into an entirely different emotion.

It was some mould. Even through the expensive fabric, he could just about picture the skinscape underneath—the firm, silky breasts and the subtle hollows he'd find below her ribcage, the bare swell of her tummy and the dip to the rise of her hip bones, and then down, beyond...

What would she be like in bed? How would it feel to have those long legs wrapped around him, her breasts peaked and firm and her eyes flickering green and blue when she lost control?

He would pay dearly to find out. It was some time since he'd had a woman, and something told him Opal Clemenger would be all woman. No one could be as passionate as she was about saving her hotels, and yet be cold and lifeless in bed. That kind of passion didn't just come with a cause. It came with character. It came from within.

No, Opal was as polished and refined as the gem whose name she bore, and just as he'd seen it in the precious stone he'd seen the fire and the flame that lurked within her, below the surface, the sparks that erupted when provoked.

And she was interesting to provoke. It was interesting to try and work out what made her tick. She needed his money, but still she treated him almost as if he was the enemy. *Peculiar.* Most women were too happy to agree with him and pander to his every need, yet she seemed happier when they were disagreeing.

It would be no easy task orchestrating her into his bed.

And he wanted her there. Wanted her lush curves bucking beneath him. Begging for more. Wild. Unrestrained. Insatiable.

And he would have her.

Maybe there was a way, a way that could satisfy them both.

She was looking at him strangely, as if she was expecting something, and he smiled to himself, knowing there was no way she'd be expecting him to make a complete turn-around. Why would she, when it was a surprise to even himself?

'Maybe there's a way we can work this out,' he said at last.

She looked confused and tugged nervously at the hem of her Chanel jacket as he continued to sit. 'I don't see how, if you're not prepared to accept less than one hundred per cent control.'

'Maybe there's a chance I will accept your conditions then,' he said.

'You will?' She sat down again.

'But only on one proviso,' he added.

He followed the bump in her neck as it moved, the gentle rise and fall of her throat, as she swallowed back her nervousness.

'And that proviso is…?'

'It's quite simple,' he started, 'and no doubt something we can both benefit from. You'll get the white knight you need to bail out your business and I'll get an interest in a six-star hotel chain that has much to offer.'

She looked lost for a while, her features searching for the answer. 'But…how is this different from the offer I made you before?'

'Quite simply, I will pay what you require and accept a forty-nine per cent share of the business. Something, I must point out, a Silvagni has never done. You only have to agree to do one thing.'

'And…and what would that be?'

He looked her squarely in the eyes. 'Marry me, Opal Clemenger. I will invest in your hotel chain, on your terms, if you will agree to become my wife.'

CHAPTER FOUR

'YOUR wife! You have to be kidding. Why the hell would I want to agree to that?' Opal noticed the turned heads, remembered where she was and sucked in a deep breath. 'I think it might be a sensible idea to conclude this matter in my office.'

In truth it was an attempt to gain breathing space. As soon as she had him in the office she was telling him where to well and truly get off. It would not be a prolonged conversation.

He followed her, too close, unnecessarily close, so that his expensive cologne taunted her, even though it was she who led the way to her modestly sized but well-appointed office.

Dammit—it wasn't his cologne taunting her. It was him. He projected an aura of power and control that filled the small space of her office and made her wish she'd thought of somewhere roomier, maybe the boardroom, for this confrontation. There was nowhere here to get away from Domenic Silvagni, and right now she wanted to be as far away from him as she could get. But first, she had to put paid to his ridiculous suggestion.

Standing with her back to the wall, she crossed her arms, all too aware of the heart hammering away inside her chest. 'My offer of a share in Clemengers,' she said, with all the calmness she could muster, 'is a serious one. I'd appreciate it if you treated it accordingly.'

He smiled from his position near the closed door, tilting his head to one side and sliding his hands casually into his pockets. Her eyes followed the movement, the fine shirt exposed, the perfect fit of his clothes all but screaming the firmness of the body beneath. She swallowed and dragged her eyes back to his face, where the smile slid away and his eyes took on a predatory gleam.

'I'm perfectly serious. You agree to marry me and I'll rescue your precious hotels. It's quite simple.'

'It's quite ridiculous!'

'And expecting me to come away from this deal with only a minor partner's share is not?' His hands flew from his pockets, sweeping through the air in a potent Mediterranean gesture as he moved closer to the desk between them. 'Surely you didn't expect me to agree to your demands so easily. Surely you would have expected me to have counter-demands.'

'But marriage? You must have some ego if you think I would be falling over myself to agree to that!'

'You would prefer, perhaps, to become my mistress?'

The shock must have been all too obvious on her face and he seemed to take a sadistic pleasure from it. 'The idea is not without its attraction...' He paused, studying her closely, his gaze searing a trail along the length of her, while he stroked his chin, as if seriously considering the idea. 'But no, I think my parents would be happier if I was finally to put a ring on a woman's finger.'

'I will be neither your mistress nor your wife.'

'You think marriage to me would be such an imposition?' He moved closer, hands on hips, until less than a metre separated them. 'You are a very beautiful woman. I see the fire in your eyes, even though you try to pretend it's not there. I think we could be very good together.'

'You seem to think, Signor Silvagni,' she whispered in almost a snarl, determined not to let him intimidate her by his proximity, 'I have some interest in you as a man. Let me put it to you straight, so there are no more misunderstandings. This is a business transaction, pure and simple. I'm not interested in your body—just your money.'

Eyebrows raised, he looked down at her, and lifted one hand, gently tracing the pad of his thumb across her lips. 'Are you entirely sure about that?'

'Oh, quite sure,' she said, when the thumping in her heart had quietened enough for her to speak. 'I never put sex before business.'

'Maybe,' he said, 'that's because you never had the opportunity.'

She shoved herself away from the wall and past him, remembering how he'd trapped her in the lift and not wanting to give him the opportunity again. Only when she was safely on the other side of the small office did she turn to face him. 'Why on earth would I see marrying you as some sort of opportunity.

I don't. Can't you see there are all sorts of reasons why your proposal would never work?'

'Such as?'

'We're practically strangers! We barely know each other.' *And what I do know about you,* she added mentally, *I don't like.*

Shrugging, he leaned against the desk. 'This is no problem. My mother and father were introduced on their wedding-day. And they are still married almost fifty years later. Of course it can work, if you want it to.'

Opal sniffed. No doubt his mother had no choice but to stay married, if Domenic's father was anything like his son. 'So maybe they suited each other. But I'm not even your type.'

'Tell me, what exactly is "my type"?'

Opal thought back to the photographs and the women adorning Domenic's arm. 'At a guess, I'd say young, blonde, thin. Maybe even simpering, if not entirely vacuous.'

He cocked one eyebrow but he'd lost some of his smug I've-got-you-now smile.

'And your type is?'

It was her turn to laugh. 'I don't have a type.'

He looked up sharply and she sensed immediately that he'd jumped to the wrong conclusion. Another time she might even find that amusing. Maybe it would even be worth having him believe it. She smiled inwardly at the thought as she shook her head. 'I've seen what marriage can do to people, how it can tear them apart. I'm not into masochism. I'm happy to leave marriage to the romantics.'

'You're scared.'

'No,' she said, knowing she was telling the truth, her mother's memories weighing heavily upon her. *Risk averse* would be more like it. And with good reason. Anyone would have to be out of their mind to want to get mixed up with the likes of a playboy. Flashes of her mother's life flared in her mind's eye: her mother, bright and beautiful and so happy when her husband lavished the smallest attention on her— a cameo of pure joy and hope that things were changing, that her love was reciprocated—only to be driven to the depths of despair when he abandoned her yet again for days on end for one of his continuous supply of young women.

While she hadn't appreciated all the sordid details, even at nine years of age Opal had felt her mother's pain, her sense of utter desolation and rejection. All her mother's love. Unwanted. Unrequited. *Wasted.* And there'd been nothing she could do.

What was Domenic looking for by insisting on this marriage? A cover for his licentious lifestyle? Or a guarantee that even if he couldn't have control of Clemengers, he would at least have control of her?

The thought brought an ironic smile to her mouth. He'd never have that, even if she did agree to marry him. And there was no chance of that. But what would become of Clemengers?

Her air of vulnerability was back. He'd seen it briefly in the office this morning, as she stood bathed in the sun's light. Now she looked younger, even more fragile. As one skilled in negotiating he recognized that look—she had nowhere to go—and it was time for him to stitch up the deal.

'I'll have my legal people draw up all the appropriate papers. We need to move quickly if the formal bid is to be lodged by tomorrow.'

'No. I never said I agreed to this.'

'You don't have much choice.'

'I don't want to marry you.'

'It's only marriage. It's not as if I'm asking you to love me.'

She drew herself up stiffly. 'There's no chance I could ever love you. No chance in the world. I think at this stage it would be expecting too much even just to like you. Given those circumstances, there's hardly any point continuing this conversation.'

He looked at her levelly for a few moments, his eyes dark and brooding. Then he shrugged and slapped his hands on his legs. 'So I can only surmise you have no wish to save Clemengers.' He lifted himself from the desk, straightening his jacket. 'So be it.'

'But the hotels?' she said, almost pleading.

'You have made your decision. McQuade can have them. He can do whatever he likes with them. I don't care.'

He'd twisted the knife with the jibe about McQuade. He could see it in her face, see it in the way her eyes widened and her skin paled as the cost of her stubbornness hit home. Good. He'd offered her the chance to save Clemengers and she'd turned it down. Now it was time to play the last card. Whatever happened now was down to her.

'Goodbye, Ms Clemenger.' His walk to the door of the office was purposeful and direct.

She watched him cross the room and knew that the future of her family's business was about to walk out of the room with him. She could save it if she wanted to. *And how she wanted to!* There were so many people's careers, their lives, their futures depending on it. The staff, fiercely loyal and proud to work at Clemengers. Her own sisters, trusting her to always do the best thing by the business. But marriage? It was crazy.

But it was only marriage! Her mind screamed at her to reconsider, to make sense of the madness, as Domenic's hand closed on the door handle. What was one wedding in exchange for the guaranteed future of Clemengers and its staff? How could she deprive them of their livelihoods? How could she face the staff, how could she face her family, knowing that she could have saved the hotels and she'd thrown the opportunity away? Was it so much to ask?

The door swung wide and in an instant Domenic was swallowed up into the hallway.

'Wait!' she yelled after him, bolting for the door. He was halfway down the corridor when he turned.

'You have something to add, Ms Clemenger?'

'If you have just one more minute…' He looked at her, then glanced at his watch. 'Please?' she asked.

Finally he shrugged his assent and she ushered him back into her office, closing the door behind them, hearing nothing but the beat of blood, frantic and pounding in her ears.

'You wanted to say something?' he prompted.

'This marriage,' she began, licking her lips, 'assuming I went along with it, that is… It would be a marriage in name only, I presume?'

'Assuming you go along with it,' he started, his voice slow and melodic and with just a hint of cultured Italian accent to send ripples down her spine, 'it will be a marriage in name…'

She let go a breath she didn't realise she'd been holding. A marriage in name only—she could cope with that. Separate lives, separate rooms. Things might not be so different from how they were now. She'd look after Clemengers in Australia while Domenic would be travelling the world. They'd hardly see each other—she'd make sure of that. She could put up with marriage on that basis. She could even put up with Domenic on that basis.

'And,' he added, dragging her thoughts away from her comfortable musings, 'a marriage in the bedroom. You will be my wife, in all senses of the word.'

He couldn't be serious! He smiled, the smoulder in his eyes revealing that he was not joking.

She turned away, face burning, trying desperately to pull her thoughts together, to somehow make sense of the madness, but all she could focus on was the pictures that sprang into her mind, images of herself in Domenic's bed, lying naked with him, limbs entangled, images that could soon become a reality.

Why had she thought for a minute that Domenic

would be satisfied with a sterile marriage? Of course he would expect sex. Hadn't he thrown the mistress role at her as an alternative?

She'd been a fool to hope that any marriage between them wouldn't extend to the bedroom, even though he had his pick of women and no doubt would continue to after any marriage. What would he want with someone like her in bed, so far removed and less experienced than his usual brand of lover, unless it was to further humiliate her?

'There must be no grounds for annulment, after all.'

Annulment. She flicked her attention back to him. Of course. Sex would seal the contract and her fate. There would be no getting away from him then, no easy way out for her and certainly no public embarrassment for him. He intended nothing more than to imprison her in a marriage that she didn't want.

And there was nothing she could do about it. Not if she wanted to save Clemengers.

She took a deep breath and tried to lubricate her ashen throat, but it was a lost cause. All moisture in her mouth, just like her hope, had evaporated.

'I agree to your terms,' she said at last, her voice a croaking whisper. 'I'll marry you.'

CHAPTER FIVE

'YOU look amazing!' Sapphy stood back to survey her work. 'Absolutely stunning. And with those few kilos you've lost recently it's a perfect fit, almost as if I designed this dress with you in mind.'

'Probably wishful thinking,' said Ruby, handing her sisters a glass of champagne each. 'It's high time one of us jumped over the stick.' She picked up the remaining glass from the tray and held it high. 'Here's to Opal Clemenger, the most beautiful bride on the planet.'

'To Opal Clemenger,' Sapphy added. 'The soon-to-be Mrs Opal Silvagni.'

Opal smiled thinly, her head pounding, and stared at the image reflected in the floor-to-ceiling mirrors lining one wall of the suite, wondering whether the woman staring back at her felt any less ill than she did right now. No wonder she'd lost weight. She'd been feeling this way for weeks, ever since she'd agreed to go ahead with this farce of a marriage. And her sisters just thought she was too excited to eat. Wrong.

But Sapphy was right about one thing. The dress she'd made up on a whim for a new line she was planning this season was divine. Strapless, with an intricately beaded bodice and a gracefully draped skirt, the champagne-coloured silk dress hugged her new shape, accentuating her curves. The pale gold full-length gloves and matching shimmering veil, held in place on her softly coiled hair with the delicate tiara her mother had worn on her wedding day, completed the picture.

'It's a beautiful dress, Sapphy. Thank you. And you both look fantastic yourselves.'

It was true. Sapphy had designed and made dresses for the two bridesmaids in a style that complemented her own dress perfectly. The rich blue silk looked sophisticated and elegant with the twins' darker hair and skin tones. How she'd managed to organise everything in the four weeks' notice she'd been given was incredible but Opal was just pleased that they could both be there.

Her sisters were more excited than she was. But then, she hadn't shared with them the finer details. They'd both assumed she'd been swept off her feet and fallen head over heels with her Italian beau. Hardly. She'd been scuttled, pure and simple. And the only thing falling was her pride, minute by minute as the ceremony time loomed ever closer.

How was Domenic feeling right now? Was he having second thoughts? Only once had she seen him since that first meeting, on his brief return to Sydney two weeks ago, when all they'd had time to discuss was business, how much autonomy the Clemenger hotels would have and how the business could be streamlined without changing its ethos.

He'd been polite during that visit. So cool and busi-

nesslike that she'd had to keep reminding herself that
this man would be her husband in two more weeks.
He was clearly the supreme businessman, and this
was just another business transaction after all. Once
he'd had her agreement, he'd moved on, saving his
energy for other, more worthy pursuits.

The only other communication between them had
been by email or post. Even her engagement ring had
been delivered by courier. He'd approached the whole
wedding scenario like a machine, making all the de-
cisions—the date, the venue, the guests. He'd done it
all with unrelenting efficiency and with a speed that
was breathtaking, not even waiting until his father had
completed his current round of chemotherapy so that
his parents could travel to Australia for the wedding.
He would take her to Italy in a matter of months, for
his parents' fiftieth wedding anniversary celebration
instead. She would meet them both then.

With no parents and few family in attendance, it
was only to be a relatively small affair. Yet still she
had been permitted to do nothing, other than to invite
her sisters. If she hadn't insisted on finding her own
wedding dress, he would have arranged that too.

Didn't he trust her? Did he think she was going to
turn up wearing jeans, for heaven's sake? Frankly, he
should be relieved she was planning on turning up at
all.

She took a sip from the glass, hoping it would calm
her nerves, but the wine tasted sharp and acidic in her
mouth and she put the glass aside. She wasn't in the

mood for champagne any more than she was in the mood for a wedding. Especially not her own.

There was a knock at the door and Sapphy answered it, returning with a small, book-sized package along with a note.

Opal took it gingerly, speculating on this latest development.

'Open it,' urged Ruby. 'It must be from Domenic. How romantic.'

'Just lovely,' agreed Sapphy. 'Who'd have thought that finding a business partner for Clemengers would result in a marriage merger as well? And to the girl who always said she was never getting married. You must have him completely wrapped around your little finger for him to whisk you to the altar so quickly. He must be absolutely crazy about you.'

Opal looked at her sisters, both of them taking such delight in this wedding, making their eyes sparkle and filling their heads with thoughts of romance and love. *If only they knew.*

Maybe she should have been straight with them; told them right from the start that this was not a real marriage but merely part of a business arrangement to save Clemengers.

But she couldn't do it. The reality was hard enough to face for herself. She couldn't bear it if her sisters knew the sad and humiliating truth—that she'd been blackmailed into this wedding. Love wasn't even on the guest list.

'Come on,' Ruby said. 'The suspense is killing me. And it's almost time. Open it!'

Opal tugged at the bow and the satin ribbon slipped to the floor. She lifted the lid and gasped. Both sisters rushed to look. Inside was an exquisitely crafted gold necklace studded the length with small opals, and with five opal pendant drops, each surrounded by diamonds to make a star. Matching earrings completed the set. As the hand holding the prize trembled beneath, the gems moved in the jewellery box, catching the light and flashing all the colours of the rainbow.

'Oh, my,' gushed Sapphy. 'That's *so* beautiful. He bought you opals.'

She could do nothing but stare. These weren't just ordinary stones either, but black opals, the rarest and most spectacular variety of the gem, their dark background heightening the colours of fire contained within.

'Wow,' Ruby said. 'They're gorgeous. What does the note say?'

Sapphy took the box while Opal opened the small envelope. A hand-written note greeted her, astonishing in its brevity. *'Wear these today. Domenic.'*

'Gosh, that's a bit brief,' said Ruby, frowning, reading over her shoulder.

She laughed and tossed the note on the sofa. If she'd had any hopes that his gift meant he thought more of her than just as a chattel he'd acquired as part of a hotel chain, that terse message would promptly have put her back in her place.

Luckily she was under no misconception that there was more to this marriage than a business arrangement so there was no way she could be disappointed.

No way she could be hurt. Feeling numb was a natural anaesthetic.

'Let's see what they look like on. Hold still,' said Sapphy as she slid the necklace around her sister's throat and did up the clasp.

Opal removed her diamond studs and replaced them with the pendants. 'How do they look?' she asked, not caring particularly but knowing her sisters would expect her to be excited.

'Oh, just stunning,' offered Sapphy. 'I was worried for a moment they might be too much with the dress, but they're just perfect. The colours add more to the outfit than I could have envisaged. Before I thought you looked like a princess. But with those on, you look like a queen.'

'You do look gorgeous, sis. Domenic won't be able to take his eyes off you.' Ruby took her arm, turning her to the mirror. 'See for yourself.'

They were both right. The gown was magnificent, but the jewels were the crowning glory. Was it too much? It seemed such a con to look the fairy-tale bride when the wedding itself was basically a clause in a contract.

She touched a hand to the necklace, noticing the colours change, the diamonds sparkle in the reflection opposite. Opals. It was a nice gesture, to be sure. But were they a gift or were they part of the job description?

No doubt the prenuptial agreement would spell it out in cold black and white. She really should have read the final draft of their contract before signing it today, but she just couldn't bear to go through it one more time. Besides, it was not as if she could pull out of the deal now.

There was a discreet knock at the door. Sapphy checked her watch and smiled. 'Grab your bouquets, girls. It's show time.'

Organ music played from inside the beautiful old chapel tucked away to one side of Clemengers. Ancient stained-glass windows transformed the late-afternoon rays into streams of coloured light. It was beautiful, atmospheric and…surreal.

Opal stood at the open doorway, her sisters behind. She would walk up the aisle alone, no father to accompany her. No one to give her away. But then she wasn't being given away. She was being bought.

She caught her breath as the strains of the Wedding March started up, her cue to start her short walk down the aisle, to the man who would be her husband. *Surreal.*

Inside the chapel she saw him, her steps faltering. He turned then and her breath stopped as his eyes snagged with hers. They said something to her, something strong and powerful and all-consuming. Something that seemed to shift the alignment of every organ inside her. Suddenly she was breathless at the sight of him, his dark morning suit complementing so perfectly the rugged line of his jaw and the collar-length flick of his hair.

Totally real!

He had an aura, a film-star presence that took her

breath away. And he was waiting for her—to *marry* him. It made no sense, no sense at all.

She started walking again, the slow march to her new life, the selfsame slow march her mother had taken over a quarter of a century ago. And her mother had been happy. Heading off to a future filled with promise, filled with love. Or so she'd thought.

And here she was, taking the same route down the aisle. But there was no pretence of love, no fabrication of a marriage made in heaven. Nothing to disappoint. Maybe she was luckier than her mother after all.

Domenic took her hand. 'Smile,' he said, and she realised she had walked down the aisle on auto-pilot, seeing none of the guests, sensing nothing. 'You look breathtaking.'

She blinked, looked up at him. Had he just said that of her? His eyes met hers and confirmed it, much more than words could do, and for the first time that day warmth suffused her veins and rushed to her cheeks.

How could he have this effect on her? She didn't want to do this, she didn't want to marry him—so why could he make her feel so good, with just one look?

'The necklace is beautiful. Thank you,' she whispered, as her sisters closed ranks alongside her.

'Not one half as beautiful as you.'

Oh, my. If she wasn't careful she might even be swept away into thinking this was a real wedding, a real marriage. And if she did, she was in real trouble.

Much better to understand he was playing a part in a play, just as she was.

A moment later the priest began the service and Opal knew she was lost.

'I now pronounce you man and wife.' The priest completed his service with a pointed look at the groom. 'You may now kiss the bride.'

Opal looked at him blankly, but a tug on her hand pulled her attention back to Domenic, who was gazing down on her with a faintly mocking expression.

'Mrs Silvagni?'

'Oh.' Then his lips descended and slanted over hers and all opportunity for a response of her own making was lost. Sensations barely known, less well recognised, welled up within her as his lips meshed with hers. It was in some ways the resumption of the kiss he'd started in the lift and yet, at the same time, it was something else completely. Something more. The way his lips moved over hers, charming hers, coaxing them to respond.

But now it was more than lips. The pressure of his urged her own to open and in a moment his tongue had found hers, had traced its outline and teased it to respond. It was hard to resist. He tasted of pre-wedding Scotch and male, one hundred per cent proof.

Most of all, he tasted of desire. Desire for her. A tremor zipped up her spine. Even through her fog of inexperience she could tell that he wanted her. It was there in his touch, in his skilful possession of her mouth.

Was this how he kissed his other women? Was this how they felt, with his arms around them, charming them with his lips, promising them with his body that the kiss was just a sample of what was to come? No doubt they appreciated the attention and welcomed his need. Maybe they matched it with their own. Whatever, he was used to taking what he wanted. *As he was no doubt planning to take her*.

Dread turned her rigid under his mouth. He would be expecting to consummate their marriage tonight, the act of sex the final signature to complete this bizarre business transaction. Then she would have no chance of escape.

But she had no choice. She'd have to do it. She'd fulfil the terms of their contract, she'd be his wife in name and in bed too, if that was what was required, but she didn't have to want him. There was absolutely nothing in the contract about that.

He lifted his head at last, his eyes questioning, his brow slightly furrowed. She blinked and looked innocently back at him. Had he sensed her coolness? Or did he just expect that she would kiss him back? Maybe he wasn't used to not getting a response. She could imagine how that might be a first for him.

The Moonlight Room on the top floor provided the perfect reception venue, the wide marble columns and stone-framed full-length doors leading to the colonnaded cloisters outside. Massive potted palms reached

metres skywards yet still fell way short of the high
opaque ceiling that allowed the filtered starlight
through. Chamber music from a four-piece ensemble
filled the room.

Crisply tailored waiting staff circulated with drinks
and hors d'oeuvres. Morale amongst the staff at
Clemengers had improved noticeably since the day
she'd announced the investment by Silvers Hotels.
Several had come up and thanked her, told her they
had stopped scouring the newspapers for the chance
of another job elsewhere in the industry, how their
own life plans could now proceed—a new baby, a
holiday, a new house.

And they were thanking her by doing everything
they could to make this wedding reception perfect.
And it would have been, if it had been the perfect
marriage to start with. She was a fraud, obtaining the
goodwill of the staff, just as she'd done with her sisters, under false pretences. It was almost impossible
to smile and accept the good wishes of the guests
under the circumstances.

Someone tapped her on the shoulder and she
turned, plastic smile in place, ready to receive another
congratulatory message. There was something familiar about the blonde in the slinky red dress, now looking her over so intently that her skin crawled under
the frank examination, but she couldn't place her. It
was no surprise she wasn't familiar with all in attendance. Like everything else, Domenic had handled the
guest list, cleverly ensuring enough high-powered

travel writers were amongst the invitees to further promote the Clemengers-Silvers deal.

'We haven't met,' came the soft American drawl, 'but I just had to come and meet the clever woman who'd finally brought Domenic to his knees.'

Opal thought she caught a hint of something less than good wishes in the woman's tone. There was certainly more than a hint of champagne on her breath.

'Thank you,' she said. 'I'm glad you could come.'

'Dommy *insisted* I come.'

That was when it hit her. The photographs! She was one of the blondes—the actress—hanging off Domenic's arm. How sweet he'd thought to invite one of his girlfriends along. Marriage was certainly not going to cramp his style.

The blonde leaned closer, as if concerned her message hadn't been understood. 'And I've *never* been able to say no to Dommy.' She took a swig from her glass, polishing off the champagne with triumph illuminating her already glassy eyes.

'Well, it's just so much easier to go along with him, isn't it?' Opal smiled sweetly at the blonde, despite feeling the urge to empty her glass all over her. 'I tried, but *Dommy* simply wouldn't take no for an answer when he *insisted* I marry him.' She shrugged and gave a lilting laugh, enjoying watching the other's face turn from victory to defeat. 'What's a girl to do? Excuse me, I must see to the arrangements for the meal. Lovely to meet you, Miss...?'

But the blonde had already left, making a direct line for the waiter and his tray of champagne.

'You haven't touched your meal,' Domenic said, leaning towards her when they were finally seated for their meal at the lavishly decorated head table. 'You should eat.'

She looked down at her plate. She'd pushed things idly around with her fork, but she hadn't had a bite of the normally appetising food. She couldn't. Even though it was so perfectly presented, so exquisitely arranged to give a blend of colour, a combination of texture and aroma she knew from her work with the chefs would be tantalising. But her senses didn't register any of it. She put her fork down next to her knife on the plate. 'I'm not hungry.'

In a moment the unwanted meal was whisked away by the staff, along with Domenic's empty plate.

'You've lost weight since I was last here.'

She looked up at him sharply. What did he expect? It hadn't exactly been a stress-free month. 'I can't imagine why.'

His eyes told her he didn't appreciate her tone. Too bad. Her headache was getting worse as the evening progressed. She massaged her temple, willing away the throbbing.

'Are you unwell?'

'No.' She shook her head. 'It's nothing.'

'We can get a doctor if you need one. I want you healthy if you are to bear me a son as soon as possible.'

Her head swam, the words not making any sense. 'What did you say?'

He shrugged, placing his serviette on the table as he swivelled around on his chair. 'You need to be healthy. If you are to provide me with an heir you will need your strength. I don't want you losing any more weight.'

'And who said I would be providing you with an heir? Just because I agreed that I must sleep with you does not mean I have to bear you a child. Frankly it will be hard enough to bear the act itself, let alone any spawn of your loins.'

She picked up her glass, seeking the refreshing iced water, anything to cool the pulse that thundered in her head. But before she could lift it, his hand snapped onto her wrist. Water splashed over her hand. He took no notice.

'I assume you did read your copy of the contract before you signed and sent it back?'

Anyone watching might have thought they were engaged in a lover's game, exchanging lovers' secrets, but then they wouldn't see the fire in his eyes, the white-hot anger that was burning up the air between them, and the pressure of his hand on hers. Her fingers lost their hold on the glass. It slipped through, falling awkwardly the few centimetres to the linen tablecloth before tipping over. She watched the water soak in, the ever expanding outline of the spill, without registering it.

The contract. The lawyer had advised the changes were minor. What a fool she'd been not to go through it clause by humiliating clause before she'd signed. As if she could trust this man an inch. 'I never agreed to have a child. That was never part of our original agreement.'

She attempted to pull back her arm, but his grip merely tightened. She winced.

'Why do you think I insisted this be a real marriage if not to have children? How else am I to give my family an heir?' He hesitated for a moment, as if waiting for his words to sink in. 'Surely you didn't imagine I was so taken with your sparkling company?'

'Not for a minute,' she hit back at him. 'At least it appears we have that much in common.'

He flicked her arm from his grip and she clutched the hand to her, massaging the stinging flesh with her other hand as she raised herself from the chair.

'Where are you going?'

'Is it also a condition of the contract that I tell you every time I need the bathroom?' His glower was her only answer. 'No? You do surprise me.' She turned to go, but not before she'd heard his muttered curse and the sound of his chair being flung back, before he stormed off in the opposite direction.

Her head pounding worse than before, Opal stood bracing her arms on the marble counter in the ladies' lounge. She didn't need to lift her head and look in the mirror to know she looked as completely washed out as she felt.

It wasn't just her head. Every part of her felt out

of sorts. Her shoulders were tight, her neck a mass of knots and an empty sickness plagued her from within.

She rolled her head, trying to lessen the tension in her neck and shoulders, knowing that even if she could ease the symptoms of her stress, there was little she could do about the cause.

He was out there, her new husband, larger than life and even more demanding.

And he was expecting her to act like his wife and perform her part in this farce, to dance with him in the bridal waltz, to jointly cut the multi-tiered cake, and the final act, to share his bed in the bridal suite upstairs.

Her breathing quickened, light and heady as her pulse raced.

Would this night never be over?

Domenic would be expecting sex tonight, a consummation of their marriage and an end to any chance she would have to escape this arrangement.

And he was a man who would unquestionably have had plenty of experience of sex. What was he going to make of her?

Would he be disappointed with her? Would tonight make him regret his hasty decision to marry her? Would her humiliation plunge to new depths in his bed?

She paced the carpeted lounge, kneading the knots in her neck with her fingers, trying to massage away the tightness.

This wasn't supposed to happen to her. She'd been the one who was never getting married, never getting involved. She'd deliberately avoided getting close to men, so that there was no chance of ever losing herself in a doomed relationship, no chance of ever being hurt.

The barriers she'd worked so hard at erecting around her life had served her well. So how was it that she found herself here today?

Blackmailed into marriage with a man who thought nothing of inviting his mistress to the ceremony. Blackmailed by a playboy.

She took a deep breath, relieved that the headache, along with the tension, had eased marginally.

There was nothing she could do but get out there and get on with it. Maybe he'd be angry with her when he found out. Maybe he'd just think his new wife a loser, unable to pull a guy without the promise of a hotel empire to go with it.

Whatever, Domenic Silvagni was about to get more than he bargained for. He was about to get himself a virgin.

CHAPTER SIX

THE bridal suite had been prepared. The room was elegant and richly decorated, the cornices adorned with cupids and bows, the curtains layered and ruched, elegantly draping over the large picture windows. Champagne chilled in a silver ice bucket alongside two crystal champagne flutes. A chocolate basket filled with strawberries completed the tray.

But it was the bed that preoccupied her. The large four-poster bed dominated the room, already prepared for its new occupants, the embroidered satin counterpane turned down, a single orchid adorning each pillow. Her silk nightgown had been unpacked and lay across the bed.

She shivered, not wanting to go closer. The bed was so big, but then again she would be sharing it with Domenic. Somehow it didn't seem big enough.

Reluctantly she forced herself to cross the room. Domenic would be up in half an hour. He'd given her this opportunity, he'd said, to prepare herself, and for that small consideration she was grateful. Although she half suspected he was happy to prolong his reunion with his actress friend in private.

Nightgown in hand, she entered the sumptuous marble bathroom, passing the large spa bath and the shower for two on her way to the long his-and-hers vanity, where her toiletries and cosmetics had already been arranged in neat rows, alongside his own smaller collection.

So this was married life. Sharing space in a bed; space in the bathroom. She scanned his few items. A silver-handled razor. Anti-perspirant. One bottle of cologne. A toothbrush. Not much, but it probably told her more about him than she'd learned in the last month. After all, what did she really know about this man to whom she'd just become bound? Little more than he was one of the most successful hoteliers in the world and a man who was more than used to getting what he wanted. Not to mention who he wanted.

Well, in a few more minutes she was bound to learn more—a lot more—whether she wanted to or not.

She sighed, weary from the day's stresses and excitement although thankful her headache had eased considerably. A shower would wipe it out completely.

She removed her jewellery, the opal necklace and earrings that Domenic had provided, and her mother's tiara, and slipped out of the gown her sister had crafted. The last of her make-up was disappearing when she felt it, the familiar cramping deep in her abdomen, the dampness in her underwear. And it was days early. The stress of this whole arrangement was taking its toll, on her body and her mind.

So much for her wedding night. A half-smile found its way to her lips. In a way it was kind of funny, though there was little likelihood Domenic would agree.

Standing under the powerful twin sprays a few minutes later, Opal let the warmth seep into her skin, relaxing flesh weary from being permanently tense, permanently on guard. With the showerheads set to pulse, the pummelling flow beat into her muscles, a liquid massage.

It was heaven. Just a couple more minutes and she'd get out, but right now it was pure indulgence standing there, eyes closed, her face under the stream so that it cascaded down her shoulders, over her breasts and back and down her legs. Everywhere the water touched felt renewed and restored. It was a welcome change of state from the trauma of the day. And she wouldn't think about tonight. It was enough now just to enjoy the refreshing play of water over her skin, temporarily sluicing away her tension, her weariness, her concerns.

'*La sirena*. A mermaid.'

Domenic's voice speared through her dream state with ruthless efficiency. Her eyes flashed open as her arms sought to cover what nakedness they could. She swivelled her head around to see him through the clear glass doors the steam had done insufficient to fog, nonchalantly leaning against the vanity, his hand at his bow-tie. He tugged on it, once, twice, and the bow disintegrated. Another tug and it slipped from under the collar, fluttering to the floor.

'My mermaid.'

She gasped, blinking as water beaded on her lashes.

She wanted to run and hide, to cover herself up, away from his gaze. Clearly he had no concerns about her state of undress. Had he planned this? She'd been expecting to don her nightgown, slip between the fine, satin-bound sheets and turn down the lights. Was that his reason for letting her go first—so he could hijack her efforts to scamper into bed, sight unseen?

'I was just finishing up,' she said in a voice that sounded far, far away. 'I'll be right out, if you wouldn't mind passing me a towel.'

'Don't bother,' he said, his hand now at the buttons on his shirt, flicking them free one by one, 'I'll join you.'

He couldn't be serious! Surely he wasn't planning on getting in? 'It's okay, I've been in for ages.' She took a step backwards, closer to the door, hoping to get as close to the towels as possible before revealing more than a view of her back. It was clear he'd already seen much more than that—how long had he been watching her?—but letting him watch…that was different.

'Stay there.'

Her eyes flicked over to him again, ready to argue. Sure they were married, but she was still entitled to some degree of privacy. But one look at him stopped her cold. She swallowed as he discarded the shirt, his bared olive skin glowing under the bathroom lighting, shoulders broad and chest firm. Dark nipples, and a darker whorl of chest hair added texture to the otherwise smooth skin.

An unfamiliar rush of temptation surged through

her. She wanted to be angry with him. She had reason to be angry with him—many reasons. But that didn't stop her frank appreciation of his body. He was beautiful, and the urge to touch that skin, to feel it pressed next to hers threatened to wipe out all rational thought.

His hands moved to his belt and her eyes followed the movement, noticing the play of muscle under his sculpted abdomen as his hands dealt with the buckle before slowly, inexorably extracting it through the loops, one by one. She gulped as it dropped to the floor and she realised what he was doing.

Stripping. *For her.*

Her mind absorbed the knowledge with panic. Her body embraced it as a gift, as heightened awareness erupted everywhere. Under the shield of her arms, her breasts lifted and firmed, their nipples budding and supremely sensitive while a curl of desire snaked deep within her, setting spot fires in her extremities.

His hands flipped the buttons of his waistband, exposing a line of dark hair descending from his navel. When he unzipped his trousers, the breath caught in her throat and she looked away, knowing the burning in her cheeks would be as obvious externally as it felt to her.

By the sounds behind her she knew the trousers were being eased down, over his hips, past his thighs. They hit the floor and she looked upwards, seeking inspiration but finding none amongst the flumes of water raining down. A moment later the swish of silk told her she'd just missed the main event.

The glass shower door rattled on its hinge, before swinging open behind her. *Wrong,* she thought, taking a deep, steeling breath.

The main event had only just begun.

CHAPTER SEVEN

HANDS closed on her shoulders sending a wave of tremors passing through her as his form pressed itself up behind hers, sharing the cascade of steaming water from the showerheads above.

She schooled herself to be as calm as she could, to be as sophisticated as she could, but there was none of that, not with his body pressing into her, his all too obvious maleness jutting hard against her, forcing her pulse into overdrive and her panic into a living thing.

'No,' she said. 'We can't—'

'Turn around,' he said, cutting her off, his voice edged in gravel, and Opal was hard pressed not to immediately acquiesce. There was something about his voice that made her want to argue with him one minute, be swept away by him the next. But she wouldn't be that easy. Not for anybody. Especially not for him.

He didn't wait for her to respond. His hands moved her shoulders, swivelling her to face him. Then he gently removed her arms covering her breasts, bringing them to her sides, until she was completely exposed before him. With the curve of his hand he lifted her chin, until her eyes met his and she trembled, recognising the unmasked desire contained within those dark depths for what it was. *He wanted her.*

And with an intense hunger she had never before known, she knew that in spite of everything, every last thing he had demanded and forced from her, she wanted him too. And that scared her more than anything.

'You are my wife,' he stated, tracing the fingers of one hand down her cheek, his touch feather-light yet scorching in intensity. Her eyelids fluttered as his hand followed the line of her throat, swept slowly across her chest, his fingers moulding to her contours. 'You have no need to hide yourself from me.'

His face dipped and slanted, and with one hand at her neck brought her to meet his mouth, finding her lips at the exact same moment his other hand captured her breast, her gasp lost as his mouth covered hers, gently inviting, pressuring hers to comply. A raft of sensations assailed her as his mouth worked magic on hers and his fingers circled the tight bud of her nipple, teasing it ever tighter, his erection pressing into her belly, firm and insistent, the water pulsing over them in sheets.

Too many sensations, too much to analyse and much, much too difficult to focus. Easier to be swept away on a tide of feelings all-consuming and totally intoxicating—so unlike anything she'd experienced before.

The kiss deepened, the hand at her neck working the angles to give him best advantage. And he used them, his tongue probing, tangling with hers as, unable to resist the onslaught of so many sensations, she kissed him back. Her hands yearned to touch, to feel the skin that had glowed, smooth and satiny, in the subtle bathroom lighting.

Tentatively at first she let them, allowing them to settle on his waist, to slide over the smooth skin, to feel the tight muscle beneath. She wanted to touch all of him, to drink him in with her hands. She wanted more. Her hands moved further, one hand fixing on the hard nub of a nipple, and it was his turn to gasp. Breath hissed between them and his mouth left hers, nipping a trail along her jaw, sliding his tongue down her neck. His hand moved to her back, arching her as his mouth reached her breast, his tongue flicking over her nipple before taking all he could in his mouth, rolling his tongue around the engorged peak. Her other breast had no time to be jealous as his hand found it, stroking, massaging, teasing.

Lightning bolts speared through her, flashes of sensation so vivid and pervasive, their target deep inside her, setting her alight. She clutched at him now, her hands clinging to his wet shoulders, her knees threatening to buckle as his mouth left one breast, only to settle moments later on the other.

Every touch, every kiss sparked off new feelings, new fires. She was out of control. Way out of her depth. With no hope of finding her way out of the maze of passion and desire he'd drawn her into.

A hand dipped below her waist, tracing a path over her stomach, finding the curve of her hipbone and trailing down. Panic flashed bright in Opal's mind. 'No,' she said, edging away.

He pulled her back in, cutting off her protest as he

claimed her mouth again in a kiss that had her senses reeling, his hand dropping again, caressing her behind as he held her close, his fingers sliding between her thighs.

'Please, no,' she said again, turning her face away from his.

'I want this. You want this,' he responded, his voice heavy with need.

'It's not a good time for me.'

He stopped, looking down at her, disbelief evident in the frown puckering his brow. 'You have your period?'

She nodded, feeling suddenly exposed, crossing her arms in front of her.

'Does that matter?' he asked.

She blinked. 'Well, if you expect me to produce the heir to the Silvagni empire, then yes, I'd say it matters. I have to say I suspect there's little chance of conception tonight.'

He reached around and wrenched the taps shut.

'You make it sound like the worst thing in the world, to have a child.'

He jerked open the glass door, pulling down a thick towelling robe from the hanger behind the door and thrusting it at her before grabbing the second and shrugging it on.

'My feelings about children are one thing,' she said, following him out into the expansive bathroom. 'But you expect me to be some kind of—' her mind frantically searched for the right expression '—some kind of *brood mare*!' She hurled the last two words out, an accusation.

He glared at her. 'If you are going to be my wife, you may as well be put to some useful service.'

'So, that is to be my fate! To live my life as brood mare to Domenic, the original *Italian stallion*. How lucky does that make me?'

She shrugged, reaching for a towel to blot her hair. And hide her face. So that was what tonight's frenetic shower activity had been about—putting her to ''useful service''. For a moment she'd almost wanted to believe he was interested in her. Fat chance. He'd merely been preparing her for planting his seed. And she'd all but ploughed the ground herself.

'How long will this last?'

'Five days, a week maybe. It just started tonight.'

'And you didn't think to tell me you were due when we made the arrangements for the wedding?'

'*You* made the arrangements. All of them. You arranged the date, the time. I had no say in any of it. Just as I apparently get no say as to whether or not I want to have your child.'

His stony face was her only reply.

'Anyway,' she shrugged, 'as it happens, it's early. I had no idea it would come today.'

He snorted. 'How convenient.'

She picked up her brush, attacking the tangles resulting from her extended shower with gusto, as if each snarl had Domenic's name written on it. 'Very convenient, as it happens. It certainly stopped you pawing me.'

'A little while ago you didn't seem quite so averse to being pawed.'

She cast aside the truth in his comment as lightly as she could. A little while ago she'd been taken aback by the appearance—and feel—of a naked man in her shower. A naked man she'd married earlier today and who'd shown her nerve-endings she'd never known existed. Little wonder she'd been carried away.

'I guess it was naïve of me not to realise you wouldn't waste any time preparing me for my maternal duties.'

'Some might not see it as such an imposition.'

'I have no doubt of that, the way some of our guests today were falling over themselves to prove to me how accommodating they can be for you.'

'What are you talking about?'

She tossed back her head. 'Your *friend* down there. The blonde in the red dress.'

He cocked an eyebrow. 'You met Emma?'

'She couldn't wait to meet me,' she said. 'By all accounts she enjoys your company immensely.'

He took a step closer, his cold eyes revealing that the accompanying smile was no more than skin deep. One hand he lifted to her neck, tracing the skin at the V formed by her robe. 'Do you know that your eyes spark fire when you are angry? Or maybe it is because you are jealous?'

She shrugged out of his reach. *Jealous!* What a nerve. As if she cared who he was with. Without a doubt there'd be plenty more Emmas in the years to come. They would come and go with monotonous regularity, while she, like her mother, would live with the passing parade as best she could.

'You kid yourself. You were right the first time. I'm angry—angry that you would flaunt you girl-friend in my face. Here of all places—*at our wedding*. I don't care what you do and who you see, but I would ask that you at least be discreet.'

A muscle clenched in his jaw. 'And you think I invited her? Emma is in Sydney promoting her latest film.'

She looked at him, dark waves in his hair still damp from their shower, and wished she could believe him. But her mother had believed her father, believed his lies and his false promises, and there was no way Opal would allow herself to fall into the same trap.

'How *convenient*,' she snipped.

He stared at her for what seemed like minutes, his eyes brooding, face all harsh angles and planes.

'Very convenient, as it happens,' he threw back at her, moving to the dressing room. 'I'm going out. Don't wait up.'

Opal rested her arms against the vanity, taking deep, ragged breaths. Outside, she could hear the sounds of drawers sliding open, wardrobes opening and banging shut. After a few minutes a door slammed and all was silent. He was gone.

Hours later Opal lay awake, wrestling with the bed-ding and eyes burning with exhaustion, yet unable to find respite in the large bed. The large, wasted bed.

Earlier its size had threatened her. Now it mocked. Her wedding night. Her wedding bed. And she was alone.

Why did it matter? It wasn't a real marriage after all. There was nothing between them but a contract and a collection of hotels. It shouldn't have mattered. Yet it did.

This was a man she was now tied to for life for whatever reason. And so far they had had no time to get to know each other, discover and share their likes and dislikes, their favourite colour, their favourite food. Basic information.

All it would take was time, to sit down and talk to each other. If this marriage was going to work on any level, they should at least be able to do that. They could have started that process last night.

Her eyes slid to the muted digital read-out yet again. It would be dawn soon and Domenic still hadn't returned. Where had he spent the night? A vision of Emma, her expression triumphant, took prime place in her mind.

She'd still been at the reception when Opal had slipped away, many of the guests still dancing to the beat of the dance band that had followed the orchestra at the conclusion of the meal. Was that where Domenic had headed? Back to the reception to find solace with his girlfriend? He would have found a willing companion, certainly.

She flipped and punched her pillow as visions of the two of them, Domenic with Emma, played out in front of her, Emma's peroxide movie-star looks contrasting with his darker Mediterranean colouring. Had he sought refuge with her—to finish what he had started so unsatisfactorily with herself?

Burned in her mind was the feel of his hands on her. His mouth on her. Never had she anticipated that anything so straightforward as the touch of another's skin against your own could feel so good. His body had felt amazing, the press of his erection making her body crave for all sorts of things for which she'd never yearned before. And he was big. She shuddered. How would it feel to take him inside her and feel his long length slide home? The thought was simultaneously terrifying and electrifying, her body humming in anticipation. He'd taken her so far but she wanted to discover more, to discover it all.

But he was somewhere else. Maybe with someone else. And she'd as good as sent him there. What had she said? 'I don't care what you do or who you see.' She might as well have given him licence.

And it looked as if he'd taken her literally.

Was he with Emma now? Making her feel the way he'd made Opal feel earlier in the shower? Was she in his arms, his mouth at her breast, his hands on her body, caressing, coaxing, filling? Was she giving him what Opal hadn't?

She pulled the pillow out from under her head, tossing it to the floor and grabbing another, shoving her head down again. She was torturing herself. There was no point worrying about what he was doing. It didn't concern her. She had hotels to run and a new manager to source for Pearl's Place after the unexpected departure of the existing one this week due to a family crisis of her own. Much more productive to spend her time thinking about matters she could do something about.

Her relationship with Domenic was set down in black and white. There was nothing she could do to change that. She was legally obliged to give him a child and she'd do it, and she'd just have to accept his lifestyle and pray that he was discreet and careful in the process.

Maybe it could work. She didn't have to end up like her mother, spirit broken and desolate, her heart and soul destroyed by a man who abused her trust and squandered the love he should have shown her on other, less deserving women.

Because there was no chance of that happening to her, no chance of being hurt by a man who didn't value her love.

She yawned and settled into the pillow, finally feeling as if she had reclaimed some sort of control in a life that was heading in directions she'd never planned.

Domenic might have a piece of paper that said he could possess her body but there was no way he'd ever possess her heart. She wouldn't let him.

Good, she was still asleep. Domenic moved quietly through the bedroom, his feet pausing before the door to the *en suite*. It was dark and quiet inside the room, insulated as it was from the early-morning sunlight and traffic noise going on below by the heavy drapes and double-glazing. Not too dark though, to make out the fan of her hair across the pillow, the arm flung back across the bed and the mess of sheets tangled around her.

So she hadn't had a good night. She should have. She'd got what she'd wanted, or rather, what she hadn't. He continued into the bathroom and flipped on the shower, stripping off before stepping under the spray, forcing himself not to think about the last time he'd been there. The last unsatisfactory time he'd been there.

He sighed. He was tired but he could catch up on sleep on the plane. Fifteen hours to Los Angeles ought to do it. It would be early morning when he arrived so he might as well get his body clock used to it.

Two minutes was enough. A rough towel dry and he padded barefoot and naked back into the bedroom, picking up the phone. Breakfast for two. Scrambled eggs, salmon, coffee—strong.

When he turned she was looking right at him. *Frowning* right at him. He smiled to himself. 'Good morning,' he said, crossing to the walk-in wardrobe, snagging the curtains open on the way. Sunlight flooded the room. He pulled down his case, bringing it back and flopping it on the bed. It landed nowhere near her but still she scurried further towards the other side, hopelessly trying to avert her eyes.

'Morning,' she responded at last, her voice shaky, tugging up the sheets to her chest at the same time.

The movement amused him. If she thought he was

going to ravish her after last night's fiasco, she had another think coming.

'What…what are you doing?'

He moved to the dresser, opening drawers and pulling out bits and pieces. 'I have to go to the States. Something's come up.' He zipped them into the corner compartment. Then he looked at her, still studiously staring at anywhere else but him. 'I didn't think you'd mind. It wasn't as if we had honeymoon plans or anything.'

Her eyes flicked over to his and he held them, watching the emotions—relief, curiosity, suspicion—flash through, all combined with a healthy dose of embarrassment as she tried not to look away. She hadn't asked him where he'd spent the night, but he could see the question lurking there, in her eyes, along with several more.

'How long will you be gone?'

'At least a week,' he said, returning to the closet. 'Should give you enough time to finalise the new marketing and promotion plan for both groups. Think you can do that?'

'Of course I can,' she insisted, fight returning momentarily to her voice.

'Good. When I come back I want you to come with me on another trip. I need to have a look at the market in North Queensland. You might as well tag along.'

He roughly folded the shirts—he'd get them pressed in LA—and then collected his few things from the bathroom.

'I see,' she said. 'Looks as if I'm "tagging along",
then. But Domenic...'

Colour flooded her cheeks. She looked as uncomfortable as she sounded, sitting up with the bedclothes
gathered like a wall around her. 'Yes?'

'Are you going to get dressed?'

The corners of his mouth hooked up as he held out
his hands palms up. 'Does my body not meet with
your approval?'

She blinked and he could see she immediately regretted mentioning the topic. 'Well, it's just that...
Room Service will be here any minute and...'

He said nothing. Just waited as she tied her words
and herself in knots.

'Excuse me,' she said at last, sliding out of the bed.
'If you're finished in the bathroom...?' Without waiting for an answer she fled to the safety of the other
room. He heard the lock being turned. She obviously
wasn't risking another experience like last night's.

He pulled on some clothes as he threw the last of
his things into the case, snapping it closed, entertained
by her reaction. She was such a mix of character—
all hellcat one minute, spitting fire and brimstone; innocent unsophisticate the next, acting like someone
ten years her junior.

Yet in the shower last night... She'd been liquid
fire in his arms, sleek and silken to his touch and
totally receptive. He could wait for their next en-
counter. There was no doubt it would be worth it.

By the time she'd emerged encased in a thick white
robe a little while later, Room Service had delivered

their breakfast and he was sitting at the table, reading the paper. He motioned her to sit, poured her a cup of coffee.

She sat down, relieved to see he'd put some clothes on at last.

'How do you have it?' he asked.

'Just milk, no sugar.'

He added milk, handed over the cup. It struck her again, the enormity of what they'd done. Here they were, having breakfast like any other married couple. Except he didn't even know how she took her coffee.

And they weren't any other married couple. It was all out of order. It was all wrong. Yet Domenic was sitting there, reading the paper as if it were any other morning in his life.

Where had he spent the night? And why this sudden trip to the States? He'd planned on staying in Sydney a week this visit. What could have happened so suddenly that he had to rush over there?

Unless it had something to do with Emma? A cold chill zipped down her spine. But what did she expect? She'd practically forced him to leave last night. And it was clear she was out of procreating action for the next few days. Why would he bother to hang around?

Part of her wanted to ask the questions, to discover if her fears were correct, but she couldn't. *Mustn't.* If she wasn't going to care—and she didn't—then whatever he did was his own private business and she should be grateful if he kept it that way.

She sipped her coffee, grateful for the warmth the fluid generated within and turning her mind to more profitable pursuits, like how she could use the rest of today. Now that Domenic was leaving she could spend some time at Pearl's Place, try and find a new manager for the place, someone firm enough but with compassion at her heart. It was more difficult than she'd expected to find anyone with the right mix of skills and attitude.

Then it occurred to her. Deirdre Hancock. She'd been retiring from Silvers and someone like her would be perfect for the job. Maybe she'd give her a call.

'You should eat,' he said, breaking into her thoughts and bearing a plate laden with salmon, eggs and toast. 'You ate nothing last night.'

She took the plate, not feeling particularly hungry, but one taste of the delicate combination returned her appetite and soon had her finishing off the serving.

'Buono,' he said in approval, putting down the paper as he rose from the table. 'It's good to see you eat. I prefer my women with curves.' He moved to the bed, picked up his bag.

Coffee-cup in hand, she raised an eyebrow. 'And I prefer my men in underwear.'

His rich laugh took her by surprise. Even more surprising was the ribbon of pleasure that curled inside her, knowing she had made him laugh.

He dipped his head as he walked past her chair to the door, dropping the barest kiss onto her cheek, leaving only the hint of his warmth, the brush of his lips on her skin.

'Not for long,' he said with a smile, before heading for the door. 'I aim to change that. *Arrivederci, bella.*'

Opal sat there, long after the door had closed behind him, reliving the feel of his lips, the scent of his cologne. And wondering how, after all that had happened, they'd managed to find such a moment.

Was he seriously planning on making her comfortable with his naked body? What if he could? He had a beautiful body, so firm and sculpted he could have been a model for a Roman god. Would it be wrong to enjoy looking at his body without blushing like a schoolgirl?

She shivered. In just over a week he'd be back and there'd be nothing to stop them consummating the marriage. Last week, even yesterday, the mere idea of making love with him had filled her with nervous dread. Somehow that had changed. Now it felt more like delicious anticipation.

CHAPTER EIGHT

ALL hell was breaking out when Opal reached Pearl's Place that afternoon. While she usually didn't get involved with the day-to-day running of the shelter, until she found a new manager she had little choice.

Two New South Wales Police vehicles, their lights flashing red and blue, met her on her arrival outside the attractive two-storey terrace in inner Sydney. She'd bought the place some time back as little more than a run-down house in a shabby area. Things had changed a lot since then. People had started buying into the area and doing up the old places, just as she'd done. Now Pearl's Place was welcoming and warm, the street classic, elegant and quiet.

Pots of climbing geraniums and vibrantly coloured bougainvillaeas greeted her arrival on a slightly sultry sunny October day that made her jeans and T-shirt stick. Her heart sank as she stepped from her coupé. Police sirens and quiet streets didn't go together.

Offering a temporary shelter for women seeking a bolt-hole always carried with it the risk of the emotions of disgruntled partners getting out of control. This time it had been a brick through the front window and a threat for more.

The neighbours were tolerant but understandably concerned for their own welfare, and she knew that if things got too bad they could force the shelter to close. Maybe it was time to find somewhere else, more open, with grounds for kids to play in and no close neighbours to worry about their comings and goings. Now that Clemengers was saved, she could spend some time working out what to do.

Inside the house, the sixteen current tenants, an assortment of mothers and children from five families, gathered around the large kitchen table that comprised the unofficial meeting room.

'I'll have to go…find somewhere else, then,' said Jenny Scott, her face etched with the tracks of tears, as she clutched a skinny child to her chest, rocking her back and forth.

Opal knelt in front of the woman, who she knew to be years younger than the forty or so she looked, and prised one hand free, cradling it in her own. 'But where will you go?'

The woman sobbed, burying her head behind that of the child, who just kept staring vacantly, her thumb firmly wedged in her mouth. 'I don't know. But I won't go back to Frank.'

'I understand,' she said, nodding, stroking the child's hair. 'Don't worry. I'll sort something out with the police.'

Opal's heart was breaking as she left the shelter, having organised extra patrols as a stop-gap measure. She had to sort something permanent out though and soon. Pearl's Place should be somewhere the women and their children could relax in safety. She didn't want to turn it into a fortress. They were already trying to escape from a one kind of prison, after all.

Would you like to read
Harlequin Presents® novels
with larger print?

ACTUAL TYPE SIZE!

GET 2 FREE LARGER PRINT BOOKS!

Harlequin Presents® novels are now available
in a larger print edition! These books are
complete and unabridged, but the type is larger,
so it's easier on your eyes.

YES! Please send me 2 FREE *Harlequin
Presents* novels in the larger print format
and 2 FREE mystery gifts! I understand I am
under no obligation to purchase any books,
as explained on the back of this card.

376 HDL ELYF   176 HDL EL2F

| | | | | | | | | | |

FIRST NAME   LAST NAME

| | | | | | | | | | |

ADDRESS

| | | | | | | | | | | | | |

APT #   CITY

Order online at:
www.eHarlequin.com

HLP-P-05/07

| | | | | | | | | | |

STATE/PROV.   ZIP/POSTAL CODE

The Harlequin Reader Service® — Here's How It Works:

Accepting your 2 free Harlequin Presents® larger print books and 2 free gifts places you under no obligation to buy anything. You may keep the books and gifts and return the shipping statement marked "cancel." If you do not cancel, about a month later we'll send you 6 additional Harlequin Presents larger print books and bill you just $4.05 each in the U.S. or $4.72 each in Canada, plus 25¢ shipping & handling per book and applicable taxes if any.* That's the complete price and — compared to cover prices of $4.75 each in the U.S. and $5.75 each in Canada — it's quite a bargain! You may cancel at any time, but if you choose to continue, every month we'll send you 6 more books, which you may either purchase at the discount price or return to us and cancel your subscription.

*Terms and prices subject to change without notice. Sales tax applicable in N.Y. Canadian residents will be charged applicable provincial taxes and GST. All orders subject to approval. Credit or debit balances in a customer's account(s) may be offset by any other outstanding balance owed by or to the customer. Please allow 4 to 6 weeks for delivery.

She sucked in a breath, feeling uncharacteristically disheartened.

There were so many different sorts of prisons. Her mother's had been gilded, six-star and luxurious all the way. Yet she'd been trapped too, in a marriage that was all wrong, that had sucked her life dry till there was nothing left but her withered, bitter core.

And now Opal herself was married. Bound to a man who treated her more as a possession than a partner. What kind of prison would hers turn out to be? What would be her sentence?

She shook her head and put on her favourite CD, turning the volume up loud and trying to banish the fears that hounded her. If she was going to do anything constructive for Pearl's Place, she'd have to shed this mood right now.

The Rocks café where she'd agreed to meet Sapphy and Ruby for a goodbye drink was buzzing when she arrived half an hour later, the tables full with locals winding up their weekend with some casual alfresco dining and tourists who'd spent a busy day on and around Sydney Harbour. The whoosh of the espresso machine filled any gaps in the hum of conversation, and inviting aromas of pizza, sizzling seafood and pasta, laced with coffee, filled the air.

Sapphy and Ruby had secured a table under the veranda, where the late-afternoon breeze brought promise of another fine day tomorrow and gave life to loose wisps of hair. Opal made her way over to the twins, grateful that her marriage had at least given them the opportunity to get together once more. Now that they all lived so far apart, catching up was getting harder and less frequent.

'So, Domenic managed to let you get away for an hour, then?' said Sapphy, rising to kiss her sister on the cheek in greeting.

'More or less,' Opal replied noncommittally, accepting a kiss from Ruby as well before pulling out her chair and sitting down, forcing what she hoped passed for a nonchalant smile onto her face. 'He actually got called away on business, so I guess the honeymoon is over.' She shrugged, brightening the smile as if this were just another one-of-those-things when in fact she knew the honeymoon had never begun.

'He's gone?' 'Where?' the twins asked simultaneously.

'Off to the States,' she said. 'Some crisis, apparently.'

'Oh.' The twins looked at each other before both intently focusing on their menus, which doubled as place-mats.

Opal studied her sisters. Outwardly they looked as bright and beautiful as usual, but there was something in their eyes, some message that had passed between them. Did they know the truth? Had they discovered that her marriage was all a sham?

In a way that would be a relief. Pretending this was a marriage made in heaven meant deceiving her sisters as she'd never contemplated before. They'd been so excited for her, had fussed and worried over her and cooed and gushed over Domenic. Would it matter if they knew the truth now—now that Clemengers was saved and it was too late to change things? Surely eventually she could live down the humiliation of having a marriage foisted upon her.

'What is it?' she asked, looking from one to another and resorting to the tone she'd always used as older sister when she wanted to tell them she knew they were hiding something.

The sisters looked up together. 'It's probably nothing,' said Sapphy.

'I could have been mistaken,' added the other twin.

'Are you going to tell me?'

Again they glanced at each other, before Sapphy grabbed Opal's hand in both of hers. 'Is anything wrong between you and Domenic?'

Opal tried to laugh, but the sound came out weak and brittle. 'Like what? Just because he gets called away on business suddenly?'

'But the day after your wedding?'

'It's an emergency. He had to go. In fact, he's taking me up to North Queensland next week, to make up for it.' She looked in their faces and it was clear they weren't convinced. There was something else they weren't telling her.

'Something's wrong,' she said. 'Tell me.'

'Well, it's just that last night, after the reception, I went down to the lobby to say goodbye to some of the guests…'

'And?'

'And I saw—well, I *thought* I saw Domenic getting into a taxi.'

'Oh.' Opal's mind whirled, working on the run. She had no idea where Domenic had gone once he'd left her. He could easily have left the hotel. 'That's right. He left some things in his suite, at Silvers. He went to collect them.'

Ruby looked at her, a frown creasing her perfect brow and pain evident in her eyes. 'Opal, he was with that film star. You know, the one at the wedding.'

Opal's mind reeled as her darkest doubts and suspicions were confirmed. He'd spent the night with Emma. True to type, he'd run straight into the arms of his waiting girlfriend. Decades could pass but nothing really changed, not when it came to the behaviour of men like him.

It shouldn't come as a shock, not when she'd known this was how her married life would be and when she'd suspected this very thing happening, but the knowledge that she'd been right carried no sense of victory. Not when the edges of that knowledge were jagged and sharp and designed to rip you apart.

She schooled her face as best she could and looked around frantically, trying to cover the crash of emotions inside her by searching for a waiter. 'You think we might get some service around here. I'm parched.'

'Opal,' said Sapphy, gently squeezing her hand. 'Is there anything we can do?'

Opal looked into their faces, full of love and concern for her, and knew she couldn't tell them the truth. She'd been kidding herself to think that it didn't matter if now they knew. It made no difference before or after the wedding—she just couldn't let them go home thinking this marriage was less than right. It wouldn't be fair to them. This was something she had to do.

'It's not what you think,' she started. 'Emma is an old friend of Domenic's and she wasn't feeling well. I asked him to make sure she got back to her hotel safely. That's all.'

'On your wedding night?' both sisters chimed in, frankly disbelieving.

'I insisted! I mean, it was so nice of her to drop by the wedding, given her schedule, it was the least we could do.'

'So what's with the story about picking up his clothes?'

'Well, I knew you guys would jump to conclusions and you did—straight away. So stop worrying. Domenic is back in a week to take me off to a tropical paradise getaway. Try practising a little bit of envy if you can.'

'You're sure everything's all right, then?' Sapphy insisted.

Opal squeezed her hand. 'I must be the luckiest girl in the whole world, having you two looking out for me. Yes, everything's fine. Now relax and enjoy. You both head home tomorrow morning and we won't see each other for ages. Let's make the most of this, then.'

A movement behind caught her eye. 'Ah, here's the waiter. You guys go first. I haven't even looked at the menu.'

Opal stood in the airport VIP lounge, hoping she didn't look as nervous and skittish as she felt. Domenic's private jet had landed and, once the landing formalities had been completed and the plane refuelled, she'd join him for their flight to Cairns.

Even though he'd been away for longer than expected, the eleven days had flown by. She'd thrown herself into the new marketing plans, working with the promotions manager and the advertising agency in preparation for the launch of the new combined strategy.

Deirdre Hancock had been enthusiastic about working at Pearl's Place and jumped straight in, taking charge and handling the residents and their needs as if she was born to it. She'd rung a couple of days ago to say that Jenny Scott and her daughter had moved into a council flat of their own and were looking forward to making a fresh start. It was good news. There was something so satisfying about seeing the women, who came to the shelter cowed and scared, leave some time later, their heads held high as they headed off with a new lease of life. It didn't always work first time, but just knowing that the safety net of Pearl's Place was there if they needed it seemed to give their confidence a boost.

All in all it had been a good few days. So long as she hadn't thought about Domenic.

The nights had been the hardest. During the day she could work on the marketing plans, talk to the staff, oversee operations. Eventually, though, exhaustion would overtake her and she'd drag herself to her suite and her bed, only to lie there and wonder about Domenic. She had tried to make herself angry with him and think accusatory thoughts about who he was with and what he was doing, but other visions interceded and instead she found herself remembering their intimate shower and dreaming what it would be like when finally he made her his wife.

Memories of his touch had plagued her, the intense sensations unable to be obliterated. The caress of his hands, his mouth on her breast, the feel of his skin, slick and hot…

And the memories had refused to fade. Instead they had taken on a sharper focus the closer his return, almost as if they were tuning her body for what was to come.

Then his email had come, instructing her to be ready for his arrival the next day and to meet him at the airport, and her gut had clenched in anticipation. Despite the matter-of-fact wording of his email, this was no ordinary business trip to far North Queensland. The timing of the trip was no sheer co-incidence.

Something more primal and elemental was at work. Domenic was coming back to claim his mate. Domenic was coming back to *take* her.

Opal hugged herself, shivering in front of the air-conditioning. Her pale lemon linen trouser-suit was chosen for more tropical climes, and even though it wasn't a cool day in Sydney she regretted her decision not to wear something warmer. She declined an offer of coffee from the steward as she ambled by, knowing that as much as she resented Domenic and all he stood for, a large part of her craved his touch again.

He stood at the entrance to the lounge, watching her pace, her arms clutching herself tightly. The long-line jacket she wore trailed softly as she walked, her hair tied in some sort of knot at the back of her head. She stared at the carpet before her but he could still make out the frown that puckered her brow, the teeth that had hold of her bottom lip. She walked on, looking to him like a caged tigress, ready to be unleashed.

Tonight he'd oblige. The last few days he'd found himself thinking about her, thinking about how he'd finish what he'd started. And tonight she'd have no excuses. Tonight he'd unleash the real Opal. Already his body stirred at the thought. He was looking forward to this.

As if aware of his thoughts, she chose that particular moment to lift her head. Her eyes snared his and he saw—no, *felt* each ripple of the tremor that passed through her, as tangible as a living thing.

She was waiting for him, he realised with some satisfaction, just as he had waited for her these past few days. And without a doubt the wait would be worth it—for both of them.

The flight to Cairns took three hours during which Domenic seemed only interested in hearing about developments at Clemengers in his absence, and progress with the new marketing strategy. There was nothing at all personal in his manner, and if she hadn't been wearing his wedding ring she might easily have imagined she was just another employee. Which in a way, she thought ironically, she was.

He said nothing of his stay in the United States, and fielded her enquiries as to how things had gone with a polite, 'Well enough.'

And yet, just for a moment when he'd greeted her

at the airport, she'd thought she'd sensed something in his eyes, something in the way he'd looked at her, something that had made her breath stop in her chest. She must have been mistaken. Maybe she was looking for things that weren't there. Maybe he just had a healthy dose of jet lag.

The plane dipped low over the coast as it descended and Opal gazed down at the islands dotting the sea, vibrant green foliage framed in white sand, some with coral reefs around azure atolls, and all surrounded by a sea of such intense blue, the whole picture one of vivid natural beauty.

When they landed in Cairns Opal expected them to make their way to the cars waiting outside, but Domenic took her arm instead, steering her around the tarmac and towards a helicopter parked at the adjacent helipad.

'Where are we going?' she asked over the whine of jet engines, the warm air rich with aviation fuel. 'I assumed we were heading for Silvers Cairns hotel.'

He shook his head. 'Not today. I thought it was time we checked out the competition. Hop in,' he instructed.

A few moments later they were rising above the airport, rotors deafeningly thumping in spite of her earphones, so she abandoned any attempts at conversation, content to take in the view. The helicopter sliced through the warm tropical sky, carrying them down the coast. There were several resort islands along the coast, she knew, but just where Domenic was taking her remained a mystery.

In a way it was exciting, she thought, to be spirited

away, transported in the modern equivalent of his steed to a secret tropical paradise by a handsome man. It was the stuff fairy tales were made of.

But this was no fairy tale.

She stole a glance at Domenic, staring down at the view of the island wonderland below, and felt a pang of regret. If things had been different...

But what if things had been different? There was no point thinking about how it might be if they'd had a chance to get to know each other before the wedding, no point wondering what life might be like if Domenic could be satisfied with just one woman. The fact remained, if he hadn't forced her into marrying him, she wouldn't have. End of story. Happy ever after didn't enter the equation.

She sighed and turned her attention back to the view. Things were how they were. She'd known that when she'd agreed, however reluctantly, to this deal. Now she just had to make the best of it.

His hand took hers and she looked up. He was indicating out of the window to a group of islands, one elongated and larger, heading up a group of eight to ten smaller ones. She knew enough about geography and the Australian accommodation industry to know she was looking down on to the Family Islands. 'Dunk Island,' she shouted over the rotor noise.

His eyebrows rose and he nodded.

'Is that where we're going?' she asked, excited at the prospect of time on an island reputed to be one of Queensland's most beautiful rainforest islands.

He shook his head. 'No, just beyond.' He pointed

to a smaller island they were already descending towards. 'There it is. Bedarra Island.'

She knew it by reputation. One of the most exclusive hideaway resorts in the country, allowing only a handful of visitors at any one time, tucking them away in luxury villas in private Robinson Crusoe locations. If Domenic seriously wanted to check out the competition, he was starting at the top.

Minutes later the helicopter landed and they were in another world. Lush tropical rainforest surrounded them, views over the azure sea unimpeded by only the occasional silhouette of a neighbouring island.

Smiling reception staff greeted them and whisked them off to their accommodation and then faded discreetly away into the vine-latticed undergrowth, allowing them to settle in.

Opal stood on the timber deck of the Pavilion, one of the most exclusive apartments, drinking in the view of brilliant blue sea, framed by rangy rainforest eucalyptus towering over huge granite boulders that tumbled to the powdery sand beach of Wedgerock Bay below.

The apartment itself was magnificent, large open plan rooms featuring polished timber floors and slatted roofs, surrounded by floor-to-ceiling windows, and all wrapped around the pièce de résistance, the decadent turquoise-tiled plunge pool set into the deck overlooking the bay. A row of jets spouted low into the water, creating its very own waterfall, and the sound, along with the rustle and sway of the bush in the gentle spring air, was mesmerising.

It was paradise.

And it was the perfect place to be seduced. She had to hand it to him; he wasn't taking any chances this time. The trouble was, it was hard not to fall victim to the spell this place was weaving. Between the luxurious apartment, the tropical outlook and the slip of gentle waves on the shoreline below, the island spoke romance.

He came up behind her and she braced herself, wondering whether he would expect her to fall immediately into the king-sized bed with him. But instead he stood alongside her, not touching, looking out over the view, his hands on the railing.

'What do you think?' he asked without taking his eyes off the view in front of him.

'It's wonderful,' she said honestly. 'The island is a total escape and the apartment—it's just superb.'

'Good,' he said with a smile, his teeth flashing as he turned to her. 'I'd hate to subject you to any *five-star mediocrity*.' His smile broadened and she laughed out loud, amazed at her own bravado and even more amazed that he'd remembered something she'd said the first time they'd met. It seemed so long ago now. 'How about a walk along the beach before dinner?'

She looked up at him, still smiling. 'That would be nice.'

Quickly she discarded her jacket and changed her trousers and sandals for some light chino cut-offs and slip-ons, joining him back on the deck. Then they walked along the track, until they came to the path to the bay. They met no one else, but then, with a hotel capacity of only sixteen apartments, guests were scarcer than the scrub turkeys that scurried through the undergrowth. They could have had the island to themselves.

The palm-fringed beach welcomed them, and they strolled from point to point of the small bay, its ivory sand stark white against the aqua-blue water lapping its edge, the line of darker blue water beyond the bay. Sails of a beached catamaran flapped listlessly, as if even sailing was too much effort on such a day.

They talked a little but for the most part they were quiet, wrapped up in their own thoughts.

And not once did Domenic try to touch her. Opal found herself wondering why. It was obvious they had not come all this way to simply admire the view, and after more than a week of thinking and dreaming about him when she should have been sleeping Opal had been mentally prepared for a more conspicuous assault.

But this slow manipulation of her senses...

By the time they'd ambled back to the Pavilion, the sun was starting to slip away and a valet arrived with a delivery of ice and a plate of canapés.

Opal accepted the glass of Bollinger he offered her without question. It was a celebration of sorts after all. A celebration of some kind of truce between them, at least for this day.

They clinked glasses and for a moment their fingers brushed and she shivered, his touch accelerating both her heartbeat and her desire.

'Are you cold?'

Far from it. She shook her head. 'No.'

'Hungry, then?'

A lot! 'Mmm,' she murmured as she sipped her wine. 'A little.'

'Then you should eat.'

But it wasn't food she wanted. Not with Domenic standing alongside, dark hair ruffled by the breeze, his white casual linen shirt undone at the neck, exposing a tantalising patch of tanned skin, and with his chinos still rolled up at the cuff from their walk along the sand, looking more like a pirate right now than a billionaire.

Right at this moment, in the balmy tropical evening, with the tree-tops swaying and the mellifluous sound of the water spouting into the pool alongside, only Domenic could fill the cravings she felt.

Dinner meant the restaurant—other people—and maybe more delay of an hour or two before they could be alone again. Before they could resume where they'd left off on their wedding night. Could she stand such torture?

'Domenic,' she said softly, lifting her eyes to his and hoping she wasn't making a complete fool of herself, 'would you kiss me?'

CHAPTER NINE

THE evening was closing fast, the way it did in the tropics, but from the light cast from the lamp over the bar he could see the colours mix and change in her eyes. She had such beautiful eyes, so expressive, and they looked up at him, expectant, hopeful. The shyness was still there but it was edged with something else, something that flared warm and real.

He'd brought her here to take her, to stamp his claim on her and make her his wife in body as in name. That had been his plan. But after seeing her at the airport he'd again seen that inherent vulnerability, the quiet insecurity that peeled years from her. And before they'd boarded the flight, he'd changed his mind. They had four nights here before they were due back in Sydney. He would take his time and do it right. By the time they returned she would be his, and unmistakably so, his seed planted deep inside.

So he'd held off, avoiding all contact with her where he could, keeping things civil, pleasant and companionable. For her, then, to make the first move was more than a pleasant surprise.

'That is, if it's not too much trouble,' she said, turning her gaze down over the darkening sea.

'It is never too much trouble,' he said, removing her glass from her hand and placing both on the side-table near by, 'to kiss a beautiful woman.'

He shifted her body away from the railing and tilted her chin with one hand. With the other he followed the line of her jaw to her hair where he plucked free the clip holding her hair, so that it unwound, falling in feathery wisps around her shoulders and face.

Her lips, slightly parted, waited for him, her eyes wide and watchful.

He groaned, deep inside, on a breath that started and ended on her name. His lips moved to meet hers and his hands pulled her closer, until their mouths meshed, warm and wanting. She tasted sweet, laced with a hint of champagne, and as her mouth moved under his she tasted of all the contradictions she was, so sure of herself one minute, so shy and innocent the next.

She matched his moves, her tongue following his lead, dancing to his tune. When his tongue traced the line of her teeth, hers followed suit, almost as if she was copying. *Almost as if she was learning.* Had her previous lovers been so inadequate? Is that why she was so reserved?

He would change that. He would make up for their failings. He could teach her all she needed to know and still she would beg for more.

She sighed in his mouth as he changed angle and he felt her hands clutching the shirt at his back, jamming her breasts in tight to his chest. Her breasts. He remembered their feel, their weight, smooth and pert under the shower, and he wanted them again.

On a ragged breath he drew back, releasing her

only long enough to take her hand. 'It's time,' he said, before leading her into the bedroom.

And she let him undress her then, in the room with the walls of glass and with only the trees to witness, whispering secrets through their branches, rustling the music of the rainforest. And as each item departed her senses heightened, until she was naked before him, nerves and desire at fever pitch. He kissed her once, very softly, at odds with the swirling passion she witnessed in his eyes, before he shed his own clothes and eased her down on the bed.

He took both her hands and kissed each of them solemnly, without taking his eyes from hers, before he swung them over her head and pinned her down, collecting her wrists in one hand. Her eyes widened and she gasped as his mouth descended over hers, and he made love to her with his mouth, his free hand roaming the length of her, setting her aflame wherever he touched.

His mouth moved to her breasts, his tongue circling the firm buds of her nipples, then drawing them into his mouth, drowning them in heat and sensation until she clawed at his back and he returned to her mouth, pressing himself along her body. Every part of her seemed to pulse, her heartbeat thrumming, playing bass to the symphony of her senses.

Feelings she'd subjugated her whole life welled up within her, a sensory overload threatening to tip her over the borders of control. He released her hands and she relished in the freedom to likewise indulge in the feeling of him. Her hands raked his body, exploring every dip and plane of his flesh, skin over muscle, tightly corded tendons, strong hips and the firm tightness of his buttocks.

They tussled on the large bed, limbs tangling as they rolled together, their skin heated and glowing in the fire of their passion.

Her hands slipped around, driven to seek that which pressed so insistently upon her, and then it was there, in her hands, rigid and pulsing with its own special rhythm. He gasped and jerked, his breath ragged and hot in her hair.

'I want you,' she said with a conviction she'd never known before, the power of her want overwhelming in its simple truth.

'As I want you, *cara*,' he whispered, his voice heavy with longing. He flattened her on her back, masterfully wedging her legs apart with one knee. But then she put up no resistance, her need to have him obsessing her thoughts, driving her to possess him inside her.

He touched a hand to her thigh, squeezing her flesh so that her muscles clenched involuntarily, beckoning him to come closer. His fingers glided between her legs, her breath catching in her throat as they brushed over the sensitive flesh. But she stilled his hand, not wanting him to discover the truth before it could not matter.

'Please,' she implored. 'Now.'

He hesitated for a second, but only for that and she sensed that he too was impatient as he drew himself up over her, resting himself at her entrance as he kissed her mouth, the press of his lips gentle yet firm, echoing the pressure below, at first just a throbbing but then more insistent, more pressing.

Nothing mattered now. Nothing but having him inside her, filling her completely and obliterating this desperate sense of need.

She angled her hips higher to accommodate him as he kissed her softly once more before raising his head and drawing back his hips. She waited, nerve-endings screaming for release, before he made one huge thrust, the momentary flash of pain forcing her head back into the bed with a cry. He squeezed her hand but already the pain was gone and he was inside her, and all she could think about was how exquisite life could be, that it would give her this experience and awaken such feelings in her.

But it wasn't over. He was moving inside her, slowly drawing back, teetering on the edge, before sliding back home, giving the sensations she'd been experiencing a whole different dimension. She started to move with him, catching on to the rhythm, lifting her hips, rocking with his movements, tightening her muscles to keep him there just a touch longer. Red-hot waves washed over her, each one building on the other.

Sweat erupted on his brow, tiny droplets clinging to the ends of his hair as it flicked over his face. His skin glowed in the pale evening light, his eyes dark and intense, taking her with him as he rocked faster and faster, slamming his long length into her as her own inferno built, each thrust further fuelling the fire inside, pushing her higher and higher.

Until there was nowhere left for her to go. With

one final penetrating thrust he pushed her over the edge of reason, the edge of control, and all thought fragmented, nothing mattered but the incandescent brilliance of the explosion of mind and body.

A second later he followed, his body pulsing into hers, until he collapsed, slick and spent, upon her, their bodies humming in the wake of their passion.

She opened her eyes, surprised to see the room unchanged, the windows, the timber, the bed—all where they had been before. And yet nothing about her felt the same. Inside, on some basic level, she was a different person.

He stroked her arm, and rolled her over onto him.

'Are you hungry now?'

'Famished,' she said, her appetite for food reasserting itself with a growl of her stomach.

He laughed and made to scoop her off the bed, pausing over something that caught his eye on the covers. She followed his gaze. Even in the dim light the smudge was unmistakable.

She'd lied to him.

'I thought you said a week,' he asserted, his brow furrowed and his eyes flashing with anger.

She nodded. 'It was. But I believe this sometimes happens when…' Her words trailed off as she struggled to find the words. In the end she didn't need to, as she saw the realisation dawn on his face.

'Then…' He threw his hands in the air. '*Merdi!* Why did you not tell me?'

'You didn't ask.' She delivered the words in as light-hearted a tone as she could muster, attempting to crack through his sudden change of mood, but the

look he threw her was dark and malevolent. She
shrugged, rolling her body away, trying to look less
conspicuous, *less naked*, on the large king-size bed.
'Anyway, does it matter now?'

His hand came down, slapping his thigh, and he
cursed again in Italian under his breath.

Then he knelt one leg up on the bed, reaching a
hand to rest on her hip. 'Did I hurt you much?'

'No,' she said, knowing straight away he didn't believe her, and so she nodded. 'But only for a moment.'

'You should have told me,' he said. 'I would have
gone slower.'

She slipped her hand over his. 'I wanted you just
the way you were.'

He picked up her hand, turned it palm up to his
mouth, and kissed it softly. Then he swept her into
his arms. 'Another shower?' she asked as he headed
away from the bed, trying not to sound too hopeful.

He laughed softly, the sound rich and deep and
edged with enough intent to make her insides curl.
'Not yet. I thought it was time for a swim.'

He carried her through to the deck, and then down
one step and into the shallow plunge pool set over
the low pandanus palms and bushes. He kneeled
down and let her float into the water, still supporting
her shoulders with one arm. She gasped at first as the
lukewarm water accepted her body, but within a moment it seemed like the most natural place to be, and
as it was set over the low rainforest, with the jets
spouting water into the side, it was like being in their
own private stream. Water spilled over her skin as

she moved, sliding off, leaving behind beads that rolled away, a silver trail in the low light.

'*La sirena,*' he said, looking down at her. 'What is it about you and water?' He kissed her then and she accepted his kiss, surprisingly already feeling her senses heighten in anticipation of more lovemaking. And she wanted more. *Much more.*

As if aware of her budding arousal, he shifted his mouth to her throat, to her breast, and with each delicious sweep of his tongue her excitement grew. Her back arched, her head dipping back into the water, weighing down her hair.

He shifted her around, so her arms rested on the step, her body a feast set out for him. He sampled more of her mouth, her breasts, sweeping his tongue down to circle her navel, setting up incredible internal pressure beyond, while his arms squeezed her closer. His hand swept over the scoop of flesh from her belly to her mound, resting as he raised his head. 'Are you still sore?'

She shook her head, not wanting to talk and interrupt the sweet indulgence he was bestowing on her. His hand dipped below her legs, parting her and gently exploring that unseen part of her. She sighed, revelling in the intensity of feeling his touch generated. Then he stopped and for a moment she felt bereft, until he was back, somehow between her legs, and feelings that she'd never imagined overtook her. She gasped, her eyelids fluttering open and widening suddenly.

She snapped them shut, trying unsuccessfully to block out the vision of his dark head—*there*—but there was no hope of escaping the erotic image and even less hope of avoiding the escalating feelings, an electric charge coiling up within her, spiralling higher and higher until she was sure there must be nowhere to go. He entered her then, filling her with his length and completing the circuit as her muscles clenched down on him, building her even higher, until on one all-penetrating thrust her world split apart, a blinding flash that shattered into a myriad of tiny sparkling lights, and she was lost.

'Thank you,' she said at last, when her breathing had resumed a more normal rhythm at last. 'I think.'

He chuckled as he nuzzled in alongside, kissing the beads of water from her throat. 'Thank you. I know.'

They lay together then, listening to the sounds of the rainforest at night, their bodies in total harmony as the water lapped around them. And she thought about her new life as the wife of Domenic Silvagni. Tonight she had become his true wife, in body as well as in name. And Domenic was a superb lover; even to one so inexperienced that much was clear. It would certainly be no hardship sharing his bed.

The next day Domenic organised a picnic hamper for lunch and they motored around the island to a deserted beach in a shaded dinghy. The sand was white and pure, the sky a clear azure-blue and the sea a sparkling aqua ribbon between the two.

They swam together, Domenic deftly discarding her bikini underwater, so that their bodies could merge in the warm water. Then they dined on sashimi, coriander chicken wings and tiny quiche and washed it down with champagne, shaded from the sun by the brightly striped umbrella above. And they made love again, sensual, languorous love, before collapsing into each other's arms on the blanket.

She thought he was resting then, like her, finding this time a rare indulgence in a lifetime always focused on the business. She'd thought it would be harder to switch off but he'd seen to that. Already Clemengers seemed a distant memory in the wake of his lovemaking.

But then he stirred and propped himself up on one elbow, promptly putting paid to her assumption that he had switched off completely.

'How did your mother die?'

She blinked, totally unprepared for the question. 'I'm not really sure.'

He frowned and she shrugged, rolling onto her tummy, running her fingers through the sand. 'I guess that sounds odd, but it's true. I was only nine years old but I knew she'd been unwell for a long time, so desperately unhappy in her marriage. And then one night I heard my parents arguing, really screaming at each other.

'Not that they didn't ever fight, mind you. There were always arguments when they were together. Or, at least, Mum would plead and Dad would shout and then Mum would cry. But this time was different. I was so scared…'

She took a deep breath, fisting her hand around the sand. 'Anyway, the very next day she tried to end it all—no one ever told me the details, I guess they were trying to protect me. The ambulance came and took her to hospital, but even then I thought she was going to be okay.'

She flung the grains of sand away, scattering them on the gentle breeze, and turned her eyes to his. 'They *told* me she'd be okay! But they lied. She never came back. And I never even had the chance to say goodbye. Dad wouldn't let us go to her funeral—said it would upset us—and he never spoke about her again.'

He reached over, weaving his fingers into hers. 'You were so young.'

'Maybe. But at least I can remember her. The twins were only four, they have no memories of her at all, only a succession of nannies from then on.'

She sighed, enjoying the feel of his hand against hers. The lesson she took from her mother's life was stark and blunt. Keep your heart, it said, never give it away. It was a lesson she'd lived her life by and it had served her well. Until now, with Domenic making her aware of sensations and feelings she'd never before experienced, finding ways through her defences.

Already she didn't hate him. Already she hungered for his touch, his embrace. How long would it be before she hungered for more?

She broke his grip and rolled onto her back, dissatisfied with where her thoughts were heading and eager for a change of topic.

'Tell me more about your parents. Are they sorry they couldn't be in Sydney for our wedding?'

'That wasn't possible. Not with the state of my father's treatment.' He rolled onto his back too. 'I told you he has cancer. He has had surgery, and now chemotherapy. Reportedly all is going well.' He sighed, long and deep. 'But I know they are looking forward to meeting you in December, when they celebrate their fiftieth wedding anniversary.'

'Fifty years is a long time,' she said. 'I can't imagine people staying together for so long, least of all happily. Surely that takes a certain kind of love?'

Suddenly he sat up. 'Who knows?' he said gruffly, studying the sky. 'It's time we were going,' he said, springing to his feet and collecting up the remnants of their hamper.

They were quiet as he steered the small dinghy back to the landing deck, and she wondered what she'd done to make him so uncomfortable all of a sudden.

But by dinner an easy companionship had returned and they chatted more easily, dining on freshly shucked oysters, Vietnamese prawn parcels and seafood dishes with an Asian accent, washed down with the finest Australian sauvignon blanc.

Two more days of Bedarra Island indulgence followed, leaving Opal feeling a confirmed lotus-eater. Clocks and time had no meaning, until it was the night before they were to leave. They'd dined and walked along the moonlit beach and then returned to the Pavilion to shower together, the expectations of another night of passion heightening their senses.

Things would be different back in Sydney, she knew. These few days had seen their relationship move to a new level—a sexual level—and a side of life she'd never imagined existed. Did he realise how much he'd changed her already?

He emerged from the shower after her, looking refreshed and glowing, rubbing his hair with the towel before tossing it into the linen hamper. She watched him pad across the wooden floor, impatient when he didn't come straight to her bed, her eyes hungry as she drank in his powerful stride, his athletic legs and firm torso. He pulled open a drawer, looping some black silk over his fingers and stepping into the light underwear.

She swallowed, unable to peel her eyes from him. There was little to the black thong, very little, but what there was was put to uncommonly good use. At the back the strap rounded his taut cheeks, forming a V and pointing down invitingly to where it disappeared into the cleft. Around the front the pouch only accentuated his fullness, rather than camouflaging it.

Her mouth went dry.

'Why are you wearing that?' she asked as casually as she could.

He walked over to the side of the bed and smiled, that loosely curved smile that made her womanly parts curl and her insides quiver. 'I seem to remember you prefer your men in underwear.'

'Not any more,' she said, reaching out her arms and drawing him down on top of her.

'Take it off.'

She woke that last morning and looked over at him, his eyes closed and lashes intertwined. Now sporting a four-day beard growth, he looked more like a pirate than ever, rugged and dangerous. And for just a few days he'd been hers. They'd shared four fabulous days and nights together, with barely a hint of friction, and just for a moment the thought crossed her mind that maybe, just maybe, they could make this work.

Then the fear returned in a harsh dump of reality. This was the man who'd spent his own wedding night with another woman. Opal was simply the woman who would bear him a child. How long would he grace her bed once he'd achieved that goal?

She swallowed back a lump of regret. She was lucky really. Things could be worse. As long as she didn't love Domenic, whatever else he did shouldn't hurt her. She couldn't pretend that it wouldn't matter—that was a matter of pride. But at least her heart would be safe.

So for now she would take whatever he was offering. He'd already shown her feelings and sensations she hadn't known existed and he'd made her hungry to learn more. She'd be a willing pupil and maybe one day, whatever else happened, their stay on Bedarra Island might represent a special time for them both. She already knew it would for her.

Two weeks later Opal stood in the marble bathroom, staring at the white stick. There was supposed to be a line. There should have been a line. She flicked on the down-lights and angled the stick under the bright glare. Still nothing.

She couldn't understand it. If she wasn't pregnant, she should have her period by now. She'd even been starting to feel different this last week or so, or so she'd thought. Maybe she'd just imagined it, wished herself pregnant. Or maybe her body was just still out of sync. Considering all that had happened the last few weeks, that should be no surprise.

She sighed. Domenic would be disappointed. But then, in reality, it was expecting a lot to become pregnant in her first month. Didn't some people take months—years, even—to succeed at conceiving a child? What if she had trouble? Her husband had certainly made a lot of assumptions in his choice of wife.

She tossed the failed home pregnancy test in the bin and studied her face in the mirror, this way and that, amazed she was even thinking along such lines. One month ago the idea of having a child, of carrying Domenic's child, had been totally abhorrent. Yet here she was, suddenly desperate to see a thin blue line materialise.

But then she'd changed, more than she could ever imagine, even though nothing seemed to show in the mirror. Marriage had made its mark, to be sure. But more than anything, Domenic had changed her. And it wasn't just the lovemaking, though that was still as earth-shattering as it had been those first few days.

No, working with Domenic had given her a new appreciation of the man. He was the consummate businessman, confident and direct and able to make a decision and implement his plans quickly and effectively. The new marketing campaign had been launched without a hitch with both hotel groups already reaping the benefits. Her choice of partner to save Clemengers and move the business forward had been well and truly vindicated.

And, while Silvers didn't have the tight-knit family loyalty of its staff that was a feature of Clemengers, it was clear he had the respect of everyone, notwith-standing he was a demanding and, at times, scrupu-lously tough boss. She had to admit to a grudging respect of him herself, a respect that only grew with their time together.

But he seemed different too, and it was difficult not to like him. Where was the playboy his reputation decreed? Where were the women? Or was he just waiting for her to become pregnant, so he could revert to type? She wanted to think not. Even though she was mentally prepared for it, somehow the idea that he would split his time between wife and mistresses now seemed anathema to her. She'd been kidding her-self to think she could live with it. She would hate it.

CHAPTER TEN

'*LA BELLA donna!*' Guglielmo Silvagni held his arms out wide, gesturing Opal into his embrace. 'You never told me your bride was this beautiful, Domenic.'

They'd barely stepped from the car and into the broad vine-covered courtyard when his parents greeted them. Opal smiled and obliged, happily stepping forward into the arms of an older, grey-haired version of her husband, accepting his kisses to each cheek. For seventy, Guglielmo still had the look of power and stood tall and handsome like his son, though it was clear, by the looser fit of his clothes, that he'd lost some weight through his recent treatment.

'However were you lucky enough to win the hand of such a prize?' he asked his son.

'He had no choice,' she said before he had a chance to respond. 'I came with the hotels. It was a package deal.'

Domenic shot her a warning look, but Guglielmo was already laughing. 'Ah, Domenic, I always thought you were a good businessman, and this proves it. But I suspect you have maybe met your match in this one. You make an old man very happy, my dear.'

She smiled up at him, his laughter infectious. 'I would rather make you happy, my father-in-law.'

127

He laughed again, the sound rich and warm, the moisture in his eyes real. 'So you do. More than you could know. What say you, Rosa?'

At sixty-five, Rosa Silvagni was still a strikingly attractive woman, elegantly dressed in a fine knitted tunic and skirt that moulded her graceful figure perfectly. She smiled and took Opal's hands in hers, her gentle eyes sparkling. '*Dare il benvenuto alla famiglia.* Welcome to the family.' Then she kissed her, as Guglielmo had done, and hugged her tight.

'*Grazie,*' Opal replied, exhausting her limited knowledge of Italian.

'But I am forgetting my manners. It is such a long way from the plane. And you look so pale. Let me have Maria bring you something to eat and drink.'

Opal wasn't sure if she needed food or drink. The long flight from Sydney, coupled with the drive from the airport to the family's country estate near Volterra in rural Tuscany, had been draining and she was still feeling the motion of the plane. She eyed the inviting, wide-cushioned chairs set off to one side and knew it would be the perfect place to rest a while until she regained her land legs.

Halfway there her world tilted and spun, her knees buckled, and she crashed to the ground.

Despite her protests that she was just jet-lagged and was making too much trouble for everyone, she was bundled off to bed and a doctor summoned. It wasn't so bad really, she thought a little later, dozing in the midst of the soft bed, the thick feather duvet warm and comforting. And at least the ground had stopped moving. The doctor came, poking and prodding and asking a few questions in broken English that only seemed to require monosyllabic answers that didn't interrupt her dream state too much. Eventually he left, closing the curtains to let her rest and she drifted into blissful sleep.

Something brushed her lips, something warm and delicious and enough to make her want more. She opened her eyes, bringing into focus Domenic, sitting at her side. He took her hand, stroking the back of it with his other.

'How do you feel?'

'Better,' she said. 'I'm sorry to be such trouble though, the moment I arrived.'

He shook his head, a gentle smile playing at his lips. 'It's hardly any trouble. In fact, I have to say my parents couldn't be more excited. The party tomorrow will be a true celebration.'

'I don't understand.'

'You don't know?' he asked softly. 'I wondered if you were just keeping it a secret. But the doctor is quite sure. You are to have a child, *cara*. My child.'

'I'm pregnant?' She flattened her free hand on her stomach. A child. *A baby*—growing inside her. Could it be true?

'He suggests the pregnancy could be as advanced as eight weeks.'

'But the test…' She'd told him about the negative result last month and, although her period had never arrived, the aches and twinges she'd been experiencing in the last couple of days had convinced her that this month again they'd been unsuccessful. Had they been signs of something else—the early development of a child deep inside her—a baby?

He shook his head. 'The doctor said these tests are not always reliable.'

She frowned. 'But eight weeks. That would mean...'

'Exactly. It would mean you conceived this child during our visit to the island, possibly on our first night together.'

She nodded vaguely, trying to take it all in.

'And now you need to rest. But I wanted to say thank you, my wife.'

He kissed her then, taking her face in his hands, and touching his lips to her brow, her eyes and the tip of her nose and resting his lips on her mouth, almost sharing breath more than a kiss.

A wave of dizziness washed over her, though whether from tiredness or the subtlety of his touch, she couldn't tell. Emotion welled up in its wake as his pleasure fed her own. She'd achieved something she thought she'd never experience and she'd done it because of him. And somehow right now it seemed the most special thing in the world. In a complete turn-around she was actually excited to be carrying Domenic's child.

Would this make a difference to their relationship? Did he feel more for her than as an accessory to a collection of hotels? Already in their time together she was starting to appreciate more and more the man that was Domenic, the man behind the ruthless façade she'd seen when he'd forced her into this arrangement. A grudging respect of his business acumen together with a hunger for him in her bed was further softening her original ideas about him. If she was true to herself she'd even have to say that she liked him, and more than just a little. *Now, there was a turn-up.* She enjoyed his company and his conversation, just as much as she enjoyed his bed.

And still he'd done nothing to prove himself the playboy she thought she'd married. There'd been not one incident, since the wedding night, when she'd all but forced him away and into the arms of another woman, to cause her to question his integrity.

And now she wouldn't force him to go anywhere. Their lovemaking was phenomenal and she relished equally their nights together when they would be alone for hours in each others arms, and the stolen moments in each other's offices, a locked door, a passionate embrace that would spin out of control until the fires consumed them both. He was happy with her as a lover. She had no doubt of that. Why would he even need to look elsewhere?

Maybe her fears of his betrayal had been misplaced. Maybe she was letting her mother's sad life dictate the boundaries of her own. Maybe there was a chance for them to make this marriage work—a real chance.

His kisses were so tender, so sweet, and his words warm and rich with emotion. This was not the reaction of a man who was simply satisfied that the terms of his contract had been complied with. Surely there was something else in his kiss?

'You have made my parents very happy,' he said, finally drawing back. 'It is the perfect wedding-anniversary present. I could not have provided a better gift.'

She tried to hide her disappointment even as despair crashed over her. That was it? He was happy with her because she'd given his parents a gift? Didn't he feel just the slightest bit happy that this was something special they'd created together, a product of their lovemaking?

'No problem,' she said, smiling thinly and adding a chirpy quality to her voice that she in no way felt. 'That's what I'm here for after all. Now I'd like to rest, if that's okay.'

He looked at her strangely, his dark eyes confused and searching. 'All right,' he said, squeezing her hand before rising from the bed. 'Tomorrow is a big day. There will be lots of people who want to meet you. So sleep now.'

And she would have if only there hadn't have been so much to think about. She was going to be a mother. *A mother!* This was no longer some clause in a contract she had to fulfil, another condition to save a hotel business and all it stood for. This was a child, growing inside. A child who deserved the very best she could provide. A child who deserved a loving family.

No way did she want that child to grow up the way she had done, much too quickly and all too aware of the tensions and discord within the home. This child should be raised and nurtured in a loving environment. It wasn't fair on the child to do anything less.

If only things were different between them. If only he could appreciate the person that she was and feel some kind of affection for her other than as just an incubator—at least just for the child's sake. Was that too much to ask?

The next day dawned sunny and mild and preparations were already well under way by the time Opal rose, feeling much more relaxed and herself, although aspects of her concerns still haunted her. At the core of it was the way her attitude to marriage with Domenic had changed completely. It wasn't just a matter of being able to get on with him, though she was thankful for that development. But she wondered why it was so important to her now that their relationship be based on more than just tolerance. Of course, there was the baby, but was that all?

For one who had sworn that he would never be able to hurt her, the question continued to puzzle.

But there was little time to reflect on things as she was swept up in the celebrations for Guglielmo and Rosa, a large and festive affair with what looked like most of the region's residents present. Which was just as well, considering how much food there was. Long, white-clothed tables were set out in the courtyard and spread full of plates of antipasto, pastas and salads. The succulent aroma of a spit-roasting lamb filled the air and laughter and conversation rang out loud.

An endless procession of people lined up to meet her and congratulate them both on their marriage and baby, news of which had spread around the gathering like lightning. In fact at times she felt more the object of attention than the happy couple celebrating fifty years of marriage together.

Domenic stood by her, one arm looped proprietorially around her shoulders, introducing her to the extended family and locals alike, and constantly asking whether she needed anything or whether she was tired. But after her long sleep and with the warm welcome of Domenic's family and friends it was impossible not to feel good in their company.

When she thought she'd met everyone there and it was finally time to take a deep breath and relax with a cool glass of lemon soda, someone stepped through the crowd to meet her. Another man she didn't recognise with a woman on his arm—

'Sapphire!' she cried. 'What are you doing here? I didn't know you were coming.'

Sapphy squealed in greeting and kissed her sister, introducing her to Paolo, a "good friend", before shrugging her head towards Domenic, her smile a mile wide. 'Neither did I until yesterday. Your gorgeous husband arranged everything, and all to be a surprise for you.'

Opal looked over to him suspiciously, his eyes frustratingly hidden now beneath dark sunglasses. 'He did?'

'Of course he did. He's crazy about you. You know that, especially now, with the baby coming. Congratulations.'

Opal looked for some sort of confirmation but his lazy smile told her nothing. How could he be so thoughtful one minute yet so divorced from feelings for her the next? What was she supposed to think?

It was so generous of him to get Sapphy here for this celebration, genuinely unexpected and sweet, and it would be nice to think that Domenic had done it out of feelings for her. *Real feelings*, not just those he knew he should display as a newly-wed and soon-to-be father. He valued her; there was no doubt of that. But the impression she'd gathered from their brief chat last night was that her role in his life did not extend beyond bed-warmer and baby-maker.

Anything else was all part of the spray-on gloss of their relationship, that others might be persuaded into believing this was a real marriage. A veneer, she had to admit with some guilt, that was as much hers in the making as his. And as much as she loved seeing her sister here, it pained her still that their families were sucked into the artifice that surrounded their false marriage.

It didn't have to be this way. Something in her mind kept telling her that there must be something she could do.

Rosa sought her out late in the afternoon, and on the pretext of showing her the garden while it was still light whisked her off from the crowd. Arm in arm the women strolled around the grounds, the older woman pointing out their fields of vines, now bare of leaves, the olive groves and the boundary of the property, clearly delineated by a row of pencil pines marching down the hillside. Eventually they came to small formal lookout, where rows of rosemary bushes circled a seat that overlooked the valley below and upwards to the next hill and the walled town of Volterra.

'Our families have lived in this valley for genera-tions,' Rosa said, sitting down and gazing over the view. 'We have a home in the city, or we can stay at any of the hotels, but this will always be home for us.'

'I can see why,' she said, feeling the restful beauty of the landscape seep into her. 'It's beautiful.'

Rosa smiled and picked up one of Opal's hands in her own. 'As you are, my dear. I want to tell you how much it means to us both that you are here. Thank you for making our celebration so special.'

'Thank you for making me so welcome. I'm sorry you couldn't make it to Sydney for the wedding.' She hesitated, searching for the right words to explain their unusual betrothal. 'Everything happened so quickly.'

'I understand,' she said, patting the younger woman's hand. 'We could not have travelled then, as you know, and Guglielmo was still having chemo-therapy. It was a difficult time. News that Domenic had finally chosen a bride cheered him considerably.'

She clucked her tongue. 'And now a baby coming too, and so quickly. We have been blessed, very, very blessed. I'm sure his recovery will be much faster now.' Opal watched as Rosa wiped a tear from one eye. 'Children are a gift from God,' she said, her voice cracking on the last word.

It was Opal's turn to squeeze Rosa's hands, saying nothing as she sensed the older woman had more to share.

'I was fifteen when I married Guglielmo. I was so nervous—it was the first time we'd met—but he was already twenty and so handsome and tall and proud that I couldn't help but fall in love with him.' She looked over, smiling. 'That probably sounds odd to you, the idea of an arranged marriage...'

Opal smiled in response, thinking that times weren't so different after all.

'...but fifty years later, we are still together, still in love. All I wanted to do was give him a happy home, surround him with babies and laughter.'

She paused. 'But it didn't happen that way. We tried and tried for years without success. I had almost given up when I became pregnant. Oh, Guglielmo was so overjoyed, he was so happy. Then six months into the pregnancy I lost the baby.' She shook her head and sniffed into a handkerchief. 'I never thought I would emerge from that blackest despair. Until the miracle happened again. I became with child and Guglielmo took no chances. I had the finest doctors, the finest medical care and a long stay in hospital, where I was allowed to do absolutely nothing.' She laughed a little, her voice brittle. 'I would have gone mad if I hadn't wanted this child so much. But eventually it was time and the baby was coming. Guglielmo was so excited. He was by my side when something went wrong and I went into seizures. They rushed me into the operating theatre, delivered Domenic by Caesarean and then battled to save both our lives. After that experience the doctors would not let me consider another child.' She sighed.

'So you understand, my dear, why news of this child is so wonderful, why your pregnancy has made us so happy. And for Guglielmo especially, you have given him the best medicine in the world. More than that, you have given him a reason to live.

'And that is why we are so happy to have you in our family. Not only does Domenic bring us a beautiful bride but also the prospect of a grandchild before long. For us this is truly the greatest gift of all—the gift of life.'

Opal smiled tightly, trying to control her own welling emotion, as she met the tear-filled gentle eyes of her mother-in-law. Unable to talk, she wrapped an arm around the older woman's shoulders and hugged her close. That one woman should have to go through such pain to achieve something that should be so natural wrenched at her heart.

It had been so easy for her—almost too easy. Yet it meant so much to Rosa and Guglielmo. This was what Domenic had been alluding to last night when he mentioned her pregnancy being the perfect gift. He would naturally know the story of his mother's battle to have children. He would understand what it meant to them both.

No wonder he'd wanted a child, writing it into the contract as a last-minute amendment. It was the action of a loving son who'd chosen her to bear his children, to deliver this gift to them. She was the one he'd selected for the task.

Something inside her swelled and bloomed. It was a heady responsibility and now, with Rosa's head resting on her shoulder, one she was so proud to bear.

She squeezed her eyes shut. How could you resent a man who would go to such lengths for his parents' happiness? How could you not love him?

Her eyes blinked open. Wherever had that idea come from?

She didn't love him!

Love didn't come into it. It wasn't part of the deal.

Sure, she'd been upset when he'd left her room last night but then she'd been emotional. She'd just learned she was pregnant after all. Maybe she'd been miffed when Domenic was more excited for his parents than for the two of them, but she didn't know their story then. It wasn't as if she was hoping for some fairy-tale ending to their own marriage.

Liar, her heart retorted, hammering its protest. Why else did Domenic seem less of an enemy and more of a friend these days? Why else did she yearn for his touch, his caress, his soft words crooning her to sleep in his arms?

Why else, if not for love?

She sucked in a breath. This wasn't supposed to happen to her. She'd promised herself for her own defence, for her own sanity, that he would never have her love, that he would never have that part of her.

But it had happened.

Rosa shifted alongside, sensing something. 'What is it, dear? Is something wrong?'

And Opal sat there trying to answer, testing the taste of new words and shapes in her mouth, words that she never thought she'd utter. 'I love Domenic,' she said softly. 'I'm in love with your son.'

Rosa chuckled and rose to her feet, kissing her on the forehead before standing straight. 'You don't need to tell me that. It's there in your eyes every time you look at him.' She took Opal's arm again and hugged her close.

'Now, let us return to the party before they all start to think we're lost.'

The next two weeks in Italy were wonderful. Opal was accepted into the family as readily as if she'd been born to it. Guglielmo appeared stronger every day, regaining the weight he'd lost and filling the space in his clothes. Rosa watched on appreciatively, smiling serenely, obviously enjoying the sense of family around her she'd always yearned for.

And Domenic couldn't have been more attentive.

He'd arranged for Opal to see a specialist in the city, who confirmed what the local doctor had determined and assured her that all was well. On the way home in Guglielmo's Ferrari he'd taken her to lunch in a *trattoria* that served them huge bowls of pasta and generous servings of crusty bread and where they'd talked about the news from the doctor and discussed names and even how many children they should have.

Domenic was already thinking ahead, planning a family with more than one child if at all possible. He wanted his child to have the companionship he didn't during his own childhood. Opal had no problems agreeing. Life without siblings was unimaginable to her. Of course this child should not grow up alone.

The irony wasn't lost on her. Here was a woman, not so long ago a confirmed spinster, chatting about family planning as if it had been the number-one thing on her mind for years.

Not that their conversations were limited to family considerations. Architecture, politics and fashion, the local hotels, restaurants and even the local markets they frequented, all of these featured as topics of their conversation. It was almost as if they were making up for the time they hadn't had to discuss issues before their marriage. They were getting to know one another at last.

Only the topic of love seemed out of bounds. There was no way she could reveal her new-found knowledge to Domenic. As it was, it was hard enough for her to accept it, but he would never believe her. After all, she was the one who had sworn she would never fall in love with him. And according to what he'd told her when their deal was struck, that had been fine by him. He didn't need her to love him. This deal was about constructing a family, providing him with an heir; there were no clauses in their pre-nuptial contract that went any further than that.

So she didn't tell him. Even if she'd wanted to, she wasn't sure she could find the words anyway. Learning about this newly discovered emotion was akin to the lesson Domenic had given her in Guglielmo's Ferrari, when she was used to driving her more modest Honda coupé. Every control in the exclusive car was in a different position, every gear shift involved different moves. It was a completely different beast. And when it all came down to it, in the case of love, she couldn't be sure she was in the driver's seat at all.

Domenic himself never spoke of love. She could tell he was satisfied the way things were turning out.

Already he'd achieved everything he'd wanted from this marriage and in the shortest possible time frame. Emotion never came into it.

Except when they were in bed. There, between the two of them, passion ruled supreme. Who needed to talk of love when you made it every night?

They spent a cheerful Christmas in Tuscany and Sapphy came down from Milan with Paolo joining her the next day. Domenic insisted that Ruby fly over for the holiday and she jumped at the chance to catch up with everyone again. And Rosa was beside herself with a festive season and a full house to celebrate.

Opal had never felt happier. Christmas had never been like this at home and so far marriage was nothing like she'd expected. Now her fears of Domenic reverting to his playboy ways seemed ludicrous. It seemed crazy, being here with his family, that she could ever have thought such a thing. Even if he didn't love her, there was no way Domenic would risk his new family, risk all he had gained and the happiness of his parents, not when family was of such critical importance to him.

Even if he didn't love her, she could at least take comfort from that.

CHAPTER ELEVEN

SYDNEY felt hot and oppressive after the green Tuscan countryside, the late-December sunlight baking walls and pavements until they steamed, and reflecting in blinding flashes off the harbour.

Opal threw herself back into work at Clemengers, more satisfied and happy than she'd been for years. All three hotels were doing well, the staff happy and vacancy levels at an all time low. And the merger had done well by Silvers too. There was a synergy emerging from the deal and already they were seeing the benefits of the cross-fertilisation of ideas between the two hotel groups.

Pearl's Place was her only real concern. Only a handful of residents remained over the Christmas period, many trying to make a go of it back at home or staying with other family. Jenny Scott and her daughter had moved back in after their block of flats had been gutted by fire. No cause had been found—it could have been as simple as one set of Christmas-tree lights too many—but the police had their suspicions. Now she was home she could keep a closer eye on Pearl's Place. Maybe even see about finding that new place, somewhere with some space, as she'd been planning.

She was still reading over Deirdre Hancock's latest report when, on a brief knock, Domenic unexpectedly entered her office, locking the door behind him. She hadn't expected to see him today and hurriedly flipped over the report as he swooped down and took her chin in his hand, holding her captive as his mouth dipped closer.

'Hi,' she whispered breathlessly in the second before his lips pressed against hers, his hand moving to her neck to pull her in close. His mouth moved against hers, a sensual dance of lips and tongue that had her pulse racing and her libido climbing with it.

She would never get used to the effect of him. Every time could be the first. Only now it was better. Now she knew how good it could be between them and it made her want him more.

His hand trailed back along the line of her jaw, his kiss turning into tiny nips as he toyed with her bottom lip. 'Hi, yourself,' he said, his voice low and heavy with want. 'Are you busy?' he asked, without moving his lips more than a millimetre from hers, so she sensed rather than heard every word as a vibration in the air between them.

The corners of her lips crooked up as a now familiar excitement crackled into life inside. 'What did you have in mind?'

'Perhaps just a little office romance?' He nuzzled into her neck.

A sizzle of pleasure zipped through her. They'd made love that morning, before breakfast, and yet already he wanted her again. Was there an end to his desire? She hoped not.

She felt herself being tugged to her feet, his hands at her waist. In a second he'd freed her silk shell from her skirt waistband and then he turned her so she was facing the desk, panting in surprise and arousal as his hands raked upwards, snaring her breasts and kneading them, slowly and rhythmically as his hot mouth sought the skin of her neck. Almost impatiently his fingers sought their way under the bra, lifting it high so that her breasts fell free into his hands, her nipples exquisitely sensitive with her early pregnancy, her breasts so full and tight. He pressed up tight behind her, and she braced her hands on the desk and wiggled against his hardness, empowered by the sensations, feeling wanton and deliciously carnal.

He'd made her like this, turned her from an inexperienced virgin into his woman, his mate, and it was pure animal mating he wanted now, the fire of his passion burning bright and dangerous and exciting her beyond belief.

He rucked up her skirt, murmuring appreciatively as his fingers found her stocking tops and the garter he'd given her for Christmas, and then his hand slipped between her legs. She shifted, giving him better access, and he growled, a low rumble that fed into her need, before dispensing with the scrap that was her thong.

His urgency charged her own, she wanted him— inside—possessing her completely. He took his hands away for a moment, she heard a zip, a swish, and he was there, butting hard against her. One hand flat on her back, forcing her down, the other between her thighs, spreading her wide and building her fever, her expectations, her desires, until with one thrust he entered her on a cry, savage and primal and oh, so satisfying.

His arms wrapped around her, taking her with him as he lunged, time and again, white-hot heat binding them together, passion escalating until the volcano inside them erupted in a shattering, all-consuming crescendo.

He collapsed over her on the desk, both of them gasping, replacing the oxygen consumed in the fire of their passion, their bodies slick and spent.

And she wanted to tell him then, tell him just how much he meant to her and how she felt about him. This man was so much a part of her now. He had forced his way into her life and then shown her how rich life could be, taught her how to make love, had even given her the promise of a child.

And yet the greatest gift, he had taught her to feel. She needed him as she needed air.

She loved him.

He eased her up, adjusting her clothing before pulling her into his arms. She looked up at him, wanting to see his eyes when she told him. *I love you.* It wouldn't be that hard to say. Her mouth framed the words but she hesitated, suddenly afraid.

What if he still didn't want her love? What if he didn't care? He already possessed her in body. Did he need to know he had her heart?

In that moment his lips took hers, sweetly and gently, and she closed her eyes and fell into his kiss, a willing casualty of her own desire.

He pulled back, smiling at her. 'So what is your opinion of office romance?'

She raised an eyebrow speculatively. 'I think there should be more of it.'

He chuckled softly, kissing the tip of her nose. 'I think I can arrange that. But it will have to wait until I return. I leave tonight.'

'You're going away? So soon?' She pulled back from his embrace. He'd said nothing about any up-coming travel and New Year's Eve was the night after tomorrow. She'd secretly planned a special dinner and a bird's-eye view of the fireworks on Sydney Harbour from the penthouse apartment. A new start for a new year. A new start for them both. 'But why?'

'I have business in London. I must go.'

'Oh.' She spun away, using the excuse of fixing her appearance in the small mirror behind her door. Of course, he was the head of a huge hotel empire. Travel was part of the job. 'Is anything wrong?'

'Nothing that need concern you. I'll deal with it and then I'll be back.'

'But…it has to be now?'

'It has to be now.'

He moved to where she was standing and held her shoulders, kissing her forehead. 'I leave in two hours. I just stopped by to say goodbye.'

'Hey, you didn't need to go to so much trouble,' she said, trying to sound untouched by his imminent departure but inwardly already feeling a huge sense of loss. 'You could have just sent me an email.'

His head tilted as his eyebrows rose.

'You do that, don't you?'

'Do what?' she asked brightly. *Falsely.*

'Make out something doesn't matter, when it does.'

'What do you mean?'

'It's clear you are not happy with me leaving. Why do you make out that it doesn't matter?'

'Who said I'm not happy about you leaving? Oh, of course,' she said, laughing, 'I'll miss the sex. But then, that's all there really is between us. Sex, and—' her hand swept down her abdomen '—this baby.'

'You say "this baby" as if it is some kind of curse. Some kind of obligation.'

She looked up at him, incredulous.

'Well, isn't that what it is? I certainly had no choice. *You gave me no choice.* A marriage I didn't want. A baby that *you* wanted. I've satisfied both conditions and now that I've fulfilled the terms of your contract—I owe you nothing more. Certainly not explanations as to how I feel.'

'Why must you bring up the contract? However it happened, we are married and you are having my child.'

'Because this marriage would never have happened without that contract. The contract, I might add, you had prepared. And this baby,' her hand rested on her lower abdomen, 'represents the fruition of just another clause in that contract. This whole arrangement is so artificial it isn't funny. There's nothing more to it than that.'

'I see,' he said, controlled and clipped and completely at odds with the heated rise and fall of his chest. 'You're right. There's nothing more to it than that.' He moved past her, unlocked the door and threw it open. 'I'll let you know when I'll be back. Maybe this time I'll just send you that email.'

Then he was gone.

Stupid! Stupid! Stupid!

She slumped, shaking and weak, into a chair wondering just what the hell was wrong with her. One minute she was going to tell him she loved him and the next she was attacking him and throwing their entire marriage back in his face.

Yet he'd agreed. There was nothing more to their marriage than a contract. His ice-cold words, 'There's nothing more to it than that,' played over in her mind. He'd had an opportunity right then to tell her if she meant anything more than just another acquisition. He'd had plenty of opportunity and he hadn't taken it. He'd told her exactly what she meant to him without having to utter a word.

Ready sex and a baby machine.

That was all she was to him. And she'd just proved how ready on her very own desk. So how could she expect him to think anything else? To think she'd almost told him she loved him! What a mistake that would have been.

She sniffed, swiping at her nose and sucking in a breath. Why was she tormenting herself? She'd known how things were going to be from day one. Pregnancy hormones were making her think things—hope for things—that just weren't going to happen.

Domenic had left and she had work to do. She crossed back to her desk, picked up Deirdre Hancock's report and sat down, attempting to focus once again on the words in front of her.

CHAPTER TWELVE

DOMENIC poured a Scotch from the decanter, one eye on the clock, waiting. Nine pm. She should be here soon. From outside came the sound of party-goers and revellers getting in the mood, some already more than halfway there by the sounds, for the big New Year's Eve celebrations in Covent Garden.

He moved over to the balcony windows of Silvers London hotel, looking down into the coloured-light festooned street below. It would already be morning in Sydney. Did Opal suspect anything? He doubted it. He'd said and done nothing over the last few weeks to give anything away. In fact he thought he'd been the perfect husband. He raised his eyebrows to the window and threw down the rest of the contents of the glass, the double malt smooth on his throat, warm in his belly. Not that Opal saw it that way.

There was a buzz at the door and he put down the glass. Good, he liked a woman to be punctual, especially one he'd been so looking forward to seeing. He crossed to the door and pulled it open wide.

'Darling Dommy,' she said, throwing her arms out to him, one hand clutching a bottle of Moet, already making her way inside the room. She wrapped her arms around his neck, embedding a lipstick-clad kiss on his cheek as the bottle collided with his shoulder blade. 'It's so good to see you.'

'Emma,' he said, his hands on her arms, sensing she'd already had a decent quota of champagne, if her bright cheeks and slurring speech were any indication. Her lips were aiming for his again, seeking the target he'd so deftly steered clear of her reach at her last attempt. He slipped her hands from his neck and found a handkerchief, wiping off the lipstick residue from his cheek. 'So how did you find me this time?'

She laughed, a false, high trill that made his teeth grate, and stepped around him into his room, fiddling with the foil on the bottle. 'I have spies everywhere. Someone spotted you at Heathrow. I knew I'd find you here. Isn't it wonderful we're both in London together and for New Year's Eve? Aren't you happy to see me?'

She dropped the foil and discarded the wire with the efficiency of a practised veteran. She popped the cork theatrically, laughing at the gush of foam before looking around frantically. 'Oh, quickly. Glasses!'

He strode to the concealed wine cupboard and pulled out one glass, holding it to the streaming bottle.

'Only one?' she asked, her eyes wide and her mouth pouty and petulant. 'Aren't you going to share a toast with me to celebrate the new year? I was so excited when I learned you were here. I'm so sick of that dull publicist of mine—couldn't wait to get away from him.'

'No, nothing for me,' he said. 'In fact, I think it would be better if you left. I'm expecting someone any minute.'

Her glass stopped, mid-swig, and she pulled it from

her lips, her skilfully blue-shadowed eyes narrowing.
'A woman?'

'As it happens, yes.'

Her eyes glinted, calculating. How had he ever
thought her attractive? Of course she was classically
beautiful and perfectly packaged, the blonde hair, the
tapered nails, the spray-on sequin dress showing way
too much leg and lashings of cleavage.

But for all her high-gloss exterior, she had none of
the colour of Opal, none of her spirit and strength of
character. None of her warm, lush curves that
moulded to him perfectly at night. He sighed. He
missed her more than he realised.

'So it's over, then, with the Australian piece. I
knew that wouldn't last.'

'My wife,' he said, taking her arm and pulling her
bodily towards the door, 'is home in Australia, expecting our first child.'

'Already!' She shrugged out of his grip, making a
sound of revulsion. 'Well, congratulations, I guess.
Let me collect my bottle and we'll have a toast.' She
lunged to where he'd left the bottle while he stood at
the door, hands on hips, waiting for her to leave.

'Are you ready?' he snapped after she'd filled her
glass and raised it to him, before taking a hefty swal-
low.

'Oh, okay, I can take a hint. Just as soon as I powder my nose. You don't mind if I just powder my
nose, do you, Dommy?'

He stood there, holding his breath, waiting for her
to come back so she could get out of his room, out
of his life.

The buzzer sounded and he cursed. He didn't need Emma here now, not when there was so much at stake. He raked fingers through his hair, his other hand on the knob. It buzzed again and he knew he couldn't risk waiting for Emma to return in the hopes of getting her out of the door before she could do any real damage. The woman outside might not wait. It had been difficult enough persuading her to come in the first place. He didn't want to spook her now, not when he was this close.

He turned the handle and pulled, and in the same instant the phone rang.

Damn. Whoever it was would have to leave a message; right now it was more important to talk to the woman standing so sheepishly at his door.

In the distance he was vaguely aware that the phone had stopped ringing, but his eyes were busy drinking in the details of his visitor. She was dressed elegantly, of medium height and still nicely proportioned, though her greying hair and softly lined skin betrayed her age a little. But it was her eyes that sealed it. They looked up at him, uncertainty clouding their greenish blue depths, panic edging them with flashes of colour.

He took her hand, knowing he'd done it.

He'd found her.

Emma chose that precise moment to make her exit, taking in the tableau in front of her, a frown undoing all the expensive work of her botoxed brow.

'Do I know you?' she said, peering at the older woman, obviously trying to unravel the mystery of how she could possibly know someone so not in her own league. Then she shook her head. 'No. I don't think so.'

Domenic wasn't about to bother with introductions, just happy for her to get out of there before the woman changed her mind and fled. He moved back to let Emma pass, getting a hefty dose of the perfume cloud she'd just sprayed herself so liberally into.

'Oh, and I answered your phone, seeing you were busy.'

'And?' he said, impatient.

'No message.' She shrugged, making her breasts almost spill out of her dress. 'Must have been a wrong number.'

She huffed and turned on her heel and took one step before turning back. 'Oh, and Domenic, I must say your taste in women is not improving.' Her lips curled into a sneer and she set off towards the lifts at an exaggerated saunter.

He was drawing the older woman into his room but there was time for one parting shot before he closed the door. 'That's where you're wrong. My taste in women has never been better.'

Opal stared at the phone in disbelief. A sleepless night, tossing and turning and twisting sheets into knots, had suddenly got unbelievably worse. She'd had two days to think about their last argument. Two days to be plagued by self-recrimination and breast-beating.

She'd been so wrong in arguing with Domenic before he left, so childish and churlish and just plain stupid. So she'd decided in the night. She'd ring to apologise and wish him a happy new year and just let him know she was thinking about him and was looking forward to his return.

And at first she'd thought they'd put her through to the wrong room until something about the woman's heady American drawl had made her skin crawl and her heart clench. Right then her sleepless night had suddenly become a nightmare.

Emma was there—*in his room*.

And she'd hung up and stared at the phone, damning it with her eyes for being the bearer of such bad news. Awful news. Devastating news.

She choked in a deep breath. Yet was it so surprising? All along she'd known he was a playboy, had known that women like Opal didn't keep someone like Domenic happy for long, especially not when they were pregnant and there was no need to sleep with them any more.

And with whom had Domenic spent his wedding night, after all? It certainly hadn't been his new wife. No, Emma had been with him then, just as she was with him now on New Year's Eve in London. That explained his hastily arranged trip, at any rate. He'd been anxious to get reacquainted with his lady-love.

The details didn't matter. All along she'd known with her head that this would happen, that no good could come of their marriage. All along she'd known that, despite whatever she felt in her heart, she couldn't change the man, the fundamental being that was her husband. She'd seen it with her mother. Now she was living it for herself.

Despair rolled her tight into a ball, rocking her in

the midst of tangled sheets and twisted dreams until she tumbled sideways onto the bed. There'd been times when she'd really thought they could make this marriage work, become a real family. There'd been other times when she was sure he was just a whisper away from telling her he loved her too, when the feeling she got from him was so pronounced, it was as if their hearts had spoken to one another.

But she'd been wrong. It had all been an act. He would never love her. He wasn't capable of it.

She couldn't stay.

She couldn't live like her mother. No way could she live with Domenic, waiting for him to come home and throw her some scraps of affection until leaving for his next jaunt, his next lover. She wasn't strong enough to live with the humiliation. If he didn't love her, she'd rather go.

Her hand found her belly, still barely apparent, tucked away under which grew her precious cargo. She had a responsibility to her child, to let it grow up in an environment surrounded by love, in a family bound by love.

No way could she subject her child to a childhood like the one she'd had, growing up in a family where love and obligation were at odds, with a mother who was so obsessed with getting her husband's attention that she sometimes forgot that her children wanted and needed hers.

She rolled off the bed and lumbered to the *en suite*, getting there just in time to duck her head before her stomach rebelled and she dropped to her knees, gagging and retching into the bowl.

*   *   *

She wasn't answering the phone, any phone. The staff hadn't seen her. But then it was noon on New Year's Day, and she could be anywhere. Except Domenic was worried. If Opal had been the one calling when Emma had picked up the call... *'Merdi,'* he whispered under his breath. That didn't bear thinking about.

It was long after midnight and the revellers had largely dispersed, the flurries of snow convincing all but the hardiest party-goers to go home.

It had been a late night. Tomorrow, or rather later today, he'd board his plane and head back to Sydney. In the meantime he should get some sleep but he couldn't, not before making sure Opal was all right.

He couldn't wait to see her, to see her face and watch her eyes light up. Soon, very soon, he thought, as he picked up the receiver yet again.

Her new bedroom was on the first floor, looking out over the street. It was small but clean, with cheery floral-print curtains at the windows and with nothing to remind her of Domenic. Deirdre had looked puzzled to see her appear with her bag on the doorstep, but one look at the younger woman's swollen eyes and she'd ushered her into one of the rooms without a second glance. For that Opal was immensely grateful. There was no way she could explain any of this to anyone. Especially when she wasn't sure she completely understood it herself.

She lay on the bed, staring at the ceiling. Thank heavens she'd never told Domenic about Pearl's Place. In the longer term she'd need to find something more permanent, but for now she was safe. By the time he discovered her secret, she'd be gone. For now, though, she could take her time and work out what she should do.

Soon she'd get out and talk with the others in the lounge and settle into the routine of the refuge, sharing in the meal preparation and clean-up, doing her bit with the chores. But that could wait just a little while. Right now she needed time alone and a chance to catch up on some sleep.

Children's laughter filtered in from the hallway. Brittany Scott. She'd been playing on the landing above the stairs, dressing and redressing a collection of old dolls. She'd adopted the space as her own special playroom and she was play-acting with them, giving them different voices. The sound was surprisingly soothing, restful.

Opal smiled to herself. She was having a child. Would it be a girl? She'd like a girl. Or maybe a boy? That would be good too. He'd look like Domenic and grow up tall and strong and handsome and then he'd go and break some girl's heart the way his grandfather had broken his grandmother's, and his father had broken hers.

She turned her face into the pillow and squeezed her eyes shut. There were too many broken hearts. Far too many for such a small planet. But why did hers have to be one of them?

Summer was on with a vengeance. The next two days were hot and humid, the sun beating down with a ferocity it saved for just a few special, scorching days. People piled into their cars and headed for the beach or the harbour, anywhere there was water and the chance of a cooling breeze. The street was quiet, those who stayed at home sensible enough not to venture into the baking hot atmosphere.

Deirdre offered to drive to Bondi Beach for the day and nearly everyone jumped at the chance. Jenny Scott stayed back, suffering a migraine made worse by the heat. Brittany wouldn't go without her mother so Opal agreed to stay and help. It suited her. She wasn't ready for crowds and fun. She was still too raw.

It was quiet with them all gone. Brittany was playing with her dolls, playing quietly on the landing so she didn't annoy her mother, who was flat out in the tiled ground-floor bathroom, trying to keep cool. Opal was in the lounge room, reading a book she'd picked out of the bookcase. It was dark inside, the curtains closed, a barrier against the heat, the hum of a fan the only sound.

It was quiet and restful and still.

A window smashed upstairs, crashing glass followed a low boom, the smell of petrol and smoke, and the heady, piercing, terrified scream of a child.

Brittany. Opal dashed halfway up the stairs, trying to reach the child, but already there was no getting through. Whatever had been thrown in had spread and done its work—the top of the stairs was well alight, the flames building in intensity, smoke coming off in thick black clouds. The smoke detector over the stairs tripped, setting off a piercing shriek. Jenny staggered from the bathroom.

'What's going on? Where's Brittany?'

Brittany screamed again and Jenny looked up, the blood draining from her face. 'Oh, my God,' she said, lumbering up the stairs. 'Brittany!' she screeched.

Opal grabbed her shoulders. 'We can't go up. Run next door,' she said. 'Call the fire brigade.'

'Brittany,' she cried, trying to push past to climb the stairs. 'My baby!'

'Go,' she screamed. 'Get the fire brigade.' Jenny stumbled down and out of the front door. Brittany was weeping now, her cries for her mother barely discernible over the thunder of the consuming fire. With the stairs blocked off by fire there was no way up. *No way down.* Her own bedroom at the front would be well alight.

'Brittany,' she yelled, her throat thick with smoke, praying the child could hear her. 'Go into your bedroom and close the door. The fire brigade is coming.'

At least she hoped they were coming. She ran out the back, coughing, and looked up. Brittany's bedroom was at the back above the kitchen. Had she made it there?

There should be sirens. Where was the fire brigade? Where was everyone? She had no idea of time, she just knew that there wasn't much. She looked around the tiny back garden, searching for something, anything that might help. An old ladder lay propped along the fence, paint peeling and rungs splintering. But it looked solid enough to take her weight. She dragged it out, wrenching it from the tangle of creeper that had tried to claim it and heaving it to the back wall. She propped it up, steadying it as best she could.

It was three feet short of the window, but at least she should be able to see something from there.

She looked around, straining her ears. Where were the sirens?

She took a deep breath and looked up. Smoke was starting to seep from the cracks around the window. She had no choice. She started to climb.

It's not that high, she told herself, trying also not to think about the wobble. *Don't look down!* Instead she focused on the window sill above, coming ever nearer. She stopped on the rung three from the top and reached her hands up the wall, grabbing onto the brick sill to support herself before risking the final ascent. She peered through the glass, there was a gap in the curtains, only slim, but she could see the door—it was closed—with smoke seeping under the bottom.

Please God, let Brittany be safe. Her eyes scoured what parts of the room she could. And then she saw a shoe, a leg. She was huddled under the bed, terrified, hoping the monster outside the door would go away.

'Brittany,' she screamed. The leg trembled but pulled in further. The door looked as if it was glowing hot and the smoke grew thicker. Any minute the fire would be in the room and upon her. She knew all the advice about not entering a burning building, but she had to do something. And she'd have to be quick. There was a child's life at stake. If Brittany were her child, she'd like to think that someone would care enough to try to rescue her.

Neighbours started coming out of their doors, curious as to the ruckus and then running around with hoses and buckets, spraying down the adjoining houses.

Still no reassuring sirens pierced the air. She was going to have to risk it. She looked around for something to break the window with, knowing she had to do it before that door came down. There was nothing, no loose bricks, no old pot plants. Desperate, she pulled up one foot, slipped off her flat slip-on shoe and smashed the heel against the glass. It went straight through on the first attempt. She strained a hand upwards, twisting the latch on the inside of the sash window, and then heaved against the frame for all she was worth, edging it up. Once she could get her fingers underneath, it came easier and she pushed it high. Smoke billowed over her.

'Brittany,' she yelled, over the roar of the encroaching fire and trying not to cough, 'I'm coming. Stay low.'

Down low, close to the floor, there would be a thin layer of breathable air, at least for a little while. There was still a chance.

But the curtains were in her way. She tugged them and they fell from the rod easier than she expected. They were more use down there, covering the shards of glass from the window. With a jump she pushed herself up onto the sill, her ears picking up a new sound over the roar of the fire.

Sirens. At last!

Should she wait? Could Brittany wait?

Now she was less than three metres from Brittany. The heat was incredible, the air super-charged as flames licked under the door. In a moment the full force of the fire would be on them.

She couldn't stop now.

On her belly she pushed herself through the window, landing with a crunch on the fallen curtains and the bed of glass. Something stuck into her but there was no time to look and less chance to see. She got into a crouch, keeping her head right down, and set off across the floor towards the bed that was the young girl's sanctuary. She called out to her, trying to reassure, trying to keep her calm and in one spot. If Brittany panicked and moved now she might not find her in the red-tinted ashen gloom.

Her head hit the bed. She ducked her arm under it, flattening herself right down, groping, searching. Until she found what she was looking for and her hand descended on a tiny ankle, a child's thin calf. She tugged gently.

'Brittany!' No response.

Panic gripped her. But she'd just seen her move. *She couldn't be dead.* She tugged harder on the leg. She didn't want to hurt her but right now that was the least of their worries as the door glowed hot, flaming around the edges.

The child was so light, she came easily into her arms, a tangle of bony arms and legs, but then sat in her arms a dead weight, Brittany's head rolling lifelessly. But there was no time to check if she was okay. She turned.

Where was the window? Everything was black and grey, choking smoke and ash. She clutched the child tightly, unable to crawl close to the floor with Brittany in her arms and battling to breathe, and struck out in the direction she hoped would lead her to the window, their ticket to life.

She had to get out. Not just for her life.

Not just for that of the child in her arms.

But for Domenic's child.

Domenic, she thought as her mind swirled and her lungs burned. *I'm so sorry!*

CHAPTER THIRTEEN

HE SAW the smoke as he turned into the suburb, his dark mood worsening as he steered the car towards the house he knew she ran as a refuge. Not being able to contact her by telephone from London had been frustrating enough, but coming back to find she'd gone had driven him completely mad.

Why had she left? Sure, they'd exchanged words before he'd left. But she didn't ever strike him as a quitter. He picked her for having more backbone than that.

He rounded another bend. It was fortunate he'd never let on that he knew of her secret. It made sense that this house would be the first place she'd run to. He noticed the dark clouds drawing closer. It must be close to her.

It was her house.

Flames escaped from the front window, lapping at the old bricks, working their way upwards in the building.

Where were the emergency vehicles? He pulled over a little way down the road and snapped open his cellphone, dialling triple zero.

'Three minutes,' the operator calmly assured him. He jumped from the car, scanning the collection of people gathered outside on the street, but she wasn't among them. He forced his way through the crowd.

165

One woman was crying hysterically, screaming and calling for someone as another supported her, holding her back.

'Do you live here?' he asked.

She looked at him, eyes wild and red, fear turning her face to a terrifying mask. She lifted her arm towards the burning building. 'Brittany,' she whimpered.

'And Opal?' he asked. 'Where's Opal?'

Her eyebrows rose, a gesture of hopelessness and she turned back to the burning building.

NO!

She couldn't be inside. There was no way in from the front; everything beyond the front door was alight. He'd have to try the back. The front door on the neighbour's house was open as they worked with hoses to dampen down their home and he took advantage, sprinting the narrow straight hallway and exiting out the back door. He looked across. Someone had put a ladder up. There were two legs disappearing into the burning building.

Her legs!

'OPAL!' He didn't wait for a response, just hurled himself over the wooden fence and across to the ladder. It shuddered and creaked, protesting at his weight, but his mind was only on getting to the top. Finding Opal.

Smoke was billowing from the window, dense and rank. No flames.. yet—but he knew smoke could be just as deadly. The sirens were coming closer but would they be quick enough? It was a moot question.

He knew what he had to do. With a heave he hoisted himself through the window.

He was in a blast furnace, the oxygen consumed by the ravenous flames of the fire beyond. If the door went there would be no hope.

'Opal!' he shouted uselessly into the inferno, the sound lost in the omnipotence of the fire. Quickly he covered his nose with a handkerchief, knowing lungs could cook from the inside in this super-charged heat.

There was no sign of her. But she had to be in this room. There was no way she would have made it through that door. He had to find her.

There was a sound—a hacking cough?—and something bumped against his leg.

Not something.

Someone.

His hand reached down and found a shoulder. Felt her convulse with coughing again and moved his hand to underneath to steer her towards the window. He pulled her up and located the child in her arms just as the door swung off its melted hinges and a wall of flame burst in.

He propped the child over his shoulder, practically pushing Opal out of the window. She was battling to regain control, he could tell, and it took a couple of attempts to get her footing, but eventually she found the rungs and somehow stumbled down. He would have sighed if he'd had more time, a possible broken leg not much to risk when your life was at stake. But behind him the beds were on fire, the flames whipping closer, and sighing was out of the question.

It was like being in hell.

No, he thought, climbing through the window and finding the ladder rungs below, *not like hell*.

Hell had been watching her legs disappear through that window.

Hell had been wondering whether he'd ever see her again.

Hell had been thinking he might not.

Just as he clambered out and ducked his head below the sill, the whole bedroom exploded in a fireball that blew out what was left of the window in a spray of flying glass, shooting out straight over his head and raining down onto the emergency services, at last arriving in numbers.

He descended the last few rungs, and felt the reassuring touch of earth under his feet. In a second the child had been taken from his shoulder, rushed to emergency care. Someone yelled, 'I've got a pulse!' and he heard, 'You're a hero, mate,' but he shook his head. Opal was the hero. She was the one who'd found the child. Without her action the child would now most certainly be dead.

Uniforms surrounded her, all frantic action and shouting. Firemen. That explained it. For some reason she'd had the idea that the man who pulled her to the window in the burning room was Domenic. Had sensed it was him. But that couldn't be right. Domenic was in London with Emma. And even if he'd been home in Sydney, he wouldn't have known where to find her.

Her mind was playing tricks on her.

The paramedics hustled her to an ambulance, plastering an oxygen mask to her face. She tasted rubber, but didn't protest, because beyond that was oxygen, pure and sweet, and that made up for everything. She sucked deeply, drawing the life-giving gas into her traumatised lungs. After a few breaths she pulled the mask away, desperate to know.

'Brittany?' she said to the paramedic, busy assessing a jagged piece of glass stuck in her leg.

'The little girl? She's alive and on her way to hospital.' He patted her hand. 'She's in good hands. Don't worry.'

A huge wave of relief washed over her and, eyes shut, she tipped her head back onto the pillow, feeling the mask being put back in place.

Brittany was alive! The loss of Pearl's Place she could get over. She'd find another house and start anew, somewhere with more space, as she'd planned. It was only a building after all.

But the thought that it might have cost a resident, particularly a young child, her life, would have been too horrible to bear. Her refuge would have been less of a shelter, more of a coffin.

She took another deep draught of the healing gas, and remembered one other thing she needed to know. She pulled the mask aside once more.

'Who was the fireman who pulled me out? I need to thank him.'

'No fireman, love,' the man said, looking around behind the ambulance and then nodding. 'That guy there in what used to be a white shirt. He one of your neighbours or something?'

She raised herself up and scanned the scene. No one in anything like a once white shirt. Then the sea of uniforms parted momentarily and her heart skipped a beat.

Domenic!

His face grimy with smoke and soot and his shirt stained and tattered, he stood brooding and impatient next to a paramedic who was stalwartly trying his best to do his job. In that instant Domenic looked over into her ambulance and magically their eyes caught and held across the distance.

And his gaze rocked her soul.

That wasn't what she'd been expecting.

She'd thought when she moved out of Clemengers that her next meeting with Domenic would be full of recriminations and accusations. She'd expected a bitter debate, an even more bitter outcome.

The last thing she'd expected was a pair of eyes that speared straight into her.

And his eyes seemed to peel everything away, the resentment over his sudden trip to London, the knife-stab to the heart at discovering he was there with Emma and the pain of realising her life had become just a younger generation's version of her mother's.

But then, he'd just saved her life.

He'd saved all three lives, as she, her unborn child and Brittany had huddled together in that fiery room.

And then he'd had the sense to save his own.

'Not a neighbour,' she said, without taking her eyes from his.

'He's my husband.'

It was good to be going home. The smell of smoke still clung thickly to them and Opal was looking forward to a long, hot bath. After a night's observation in hospital they'd been released, travelling back together to Clemengers in near silence.

Hospital had been no place to talk, both of them sensing that something more than simply expressing relief that they were alive could not be achieved with all the constant coming and going of the nursing staff.

So they'd talked about Brittany and how she was progressing. He'd even helped her arrange other temporary accommodation for the now homeless residents, not batting an eyelid when Deirdre Hancock came in to take charge of the arrangements and told them both they should be resting.

But they'd both skirted around the big questions they knew would have to be answered at some stage. Those would have to wait until they were alone.

It was just before reaching Clemengers that Domenic took her hand. She looked at him, surprised, as they'd sat chastely on opposite sides of the wide seat all the way home.

'Opal,' he said, 'I brought someone back from London with me. She wanted to come to the hospital but I made her wait at the hotel.'

She stiffened and closed her eyes. Oh, God. *Please not Emma.* They'd been in London together. Surely he wouldn't bring her back here. Surely he wouldn't be that cruel.

'Who is it?' she asked at last.

The car pulled into the hotel's driveway. 'In a few moments you will see for yourself. I know you need to get cleaned up, but she's very anxious to meet you.'

Sebastian pulled the car door open wide, nodding a greeting that was lost on her, and Domenic ushered her inside, his arm tight around her shoulders, leading her through to a private lounge.

After the bright sun outside it took a moment for her eyes to adjust to the darker interior. There was a woman sitting inside. She rose from her chair, took a tentative step towards Opal.

Opal halted and blinked.

And then time slipped, a glacier of years and memories melting down to a torrent of incomprehensibility.

The woman came closer and lifted her hands. 'Opal,' she said shakily, tears welling in her eyes. 'It's a dream come true to see you again.'

Opal looked at the older woman, searching her face, recognising, knowing that she was staring but unable to stop herself.

'Mother...?' she said.

CHAPTER FOURTEEN

AND then they were in each other's arms, simultaneously laughing and crying and washing away with their tears the pain of their long separation.

They sat down together on the chaise longue, Domenic leaning against the mantle and giving the two women the space to get reacquainted.

'But how?' Opal was able to ask at last. 'All this time we believed you were dead. Where were you?'

'I know,' she said, taking her daughter's hands into her own. 'There is so much to explain and you have much to blame me for. But let me say that leaving my children was the hardest thing I have ever done in my life.'

'How could you do it?' Opal demanded, the pain of those first few months flooding back. 'The twins were only four. They cried themselves to sleep for months. They needed you. We all needed you.'

Pearl rocked her body, biting down hard on her lips as fresh tears squeezed from her eyes. 'And I thought of you all, every day, but I had no choice. He gave me no choice.'

'My father?'

Pearl nodded.

'I knew you weren't happy together, but how could he make you leave, and leave us behind? I don't understand.'

'It was my fault,' the older woman began. 'I wasn't happy. Your father didn't love me, was happy to flaunt his many other lovers in my face, and I couldn't deal with it any more.'

'So you left?' Opal said.

'Hush. Hear me out. There's more.' She dabbed at her eyes with a handkerchief and took a breath, as if collecting her thoughts.

'I was wildly jealous. I loved your father so much, while he took me for granted. Wanting him to love me consumed my whole life. I think it must have become a form of madness.

'I hatched a plan to make him notice me. I would take a lover. I planned to drive him mad with jealousy and show him that if he didn't want me then I could easily find someone who did, someone who would give him a taste of his own medicine. I found the most handsome young man in the hotel and seduced him. Just as I'd planned, your father found us in bed together.'

She paused.

'What happened?' prompted Opal.

Pearl's eyes were dim with tears and edged with the pain she must have felt then. 'He laughed. He stood there and laughed and laughed, as if it was the funniest thing he'd ever seen. And he said to my lover that anyone who chose to go to bed with me was either drunk or stupid or unlucky enough to be my husband and that position was taken, so which of the others was he?

'The young man fled, your father's laughter ringing in his ears. So I hit him. As hard as I could, trying to inflict hurt on him like he'd been hurting me for years. I hit him and hit him, trying to get him to feel something. And he did. That's when he finally got angry—we had a terrible row.' She shook her head. 'Just terrible.'

'And the next day…' Opal trailed off, remembering the terrible sounds of that night and what it had led to as if it were yesterday.

Pearl nodded. 'I couldn't take any more. He made me feel utterly worthless. I had to get out, and there seemed only one way left…'

She gave a harsh laugh. 'But I couldn't even do that right. A cleaner found me. She's the one who called the ambulance. I'm not sure your father would have bothered.'

'He told us you'd died at the hospital.'

'I know. He told me never to try to contact you girls and I never did. It was so difficult but I knew I hadn't been a good mother. I thought you might be better off without me, the state I was in.'

Opal thought to herself for a moment. 'No wonder he'd never married again—he wasn't ever free. But still, how did he get away with it, to pull off such a deception, to convince everyone you were dead?'

Pearl shrugged. 'It wouldn't have been too difficult. My parents were dead; I had no living family aside from you children. Most of my friends were in Melbourne, where we'd originally met, though I was out of touch with them by that time anyway. He would have used the excuse of a small, private cremation, no doubt, and people would have accepted that was the way he had to grieve.'

'And he wouldn't let us go—I thought he was protecting us—but there probably never was a service at all.'

'Maybe not. Meanwhile he was organising my way out of the country. He sent me to England, where I spent a long time in a private clinic. Eventually I settled in a small village outside London, and started a jewellery business with the money he settled on me.'

She smiled as she remembered. 'That way, if I couldn't see you girls, I could at least be able to work with your namesakes, sapphires, rubies and opals, the precious gems that would remind me of my daughters every day. So you were never far from my thoughts, believe me.'

'Did you know he'd died?'

She nodded and sighed, long and sad. 'I heard. His solicitor called to let me know. I thought about you even more after that. I even picked up the phone at one stage, wanting to call you. But I couldn't do it. I couldn't just walk back into your lives after so many years. That wouldn't have been fair. And, after everything that had happened, I was so afraid that you'd hate me for it.'

'How could I ever hate you? I missed you. We all missed you.' Opal sniffed, gave a thin smile. 'But you're back. You're here now.'

She patted her daughter on the hand. 'Only because your husband is one very skilled negotiator. Still, it took him all New Year's Eve to convince me.'

Opal's eyes flashed over to him. 'New Year's Eve?'

'Yes, of course. That's when I agreed to meet with

him in London. And when I had told him for what seemed like the hundredth time that there was no way I would turn your life upside down by coming back to Australia, he told me about you. How you'd set up a shelter for women who were trapped in relationships with nowhere to go, nowhere to run. That you'd named it after me.' She paused, her lashes damp, her eyes creased, but with a smile that made her whole face glow. 'Do you have any idea what that meant to me? And then there was no way I couldn't come back. Not after learning that.'

She slid an arm round Opal's back, squeezing her, a short, sharp hug.

'And to think I'd come all this way, only to be cheated out of seeing you by a fire in that very refuge.' She shook her head. 'I was so sorry to hear of the fire and the loss of the building, especially when it meant so much to you and to the families who needed it. But I'm so relieved you saved that child and got out safely yourselves.'

Opal smiled. 'I'll find another place. In fact, I think the neighbours will insist on it now.'

'Then I'd like to help,' Pearl said, 'if you'll let me.'

'You would?'

'I think I owe it to you. There's so much I need to make up for and so much I didn't do for you and your sisters when you were growing up. Maybe it will help you forgive me for abandoning you at such a young age.'

'You don't have to buy my forgiveness, but thank you,' she said. 'It would be wonderful to have your help.'

The telephone burred softly behind them. Domenic reached over and took the call, speaking softly but mostly listening.

'Who was it?' Opal asked when he'd replaced the receiver at last.

'The police have arrested Frank Scott for arson. Apparently he's also admitted to lighting the fire at the block of units where Jenny was staying previously. Sounds as if he'll be locked away for quite some time. The good news is that it sounds as though Brittany is going to make a full recovery.'

'So Jenny and Brittany can move home,' Opal mused.

'And be safe, by the sounds,' added Pearl, patting herself on the knees before rising. 'Now, I know you two need to get cleaned up properly and rest after yesterday's excitement. I'll leave you to it.'

They agreed to meet again for dinner that night. Meanwhile Domenic led Opal by the hand to their suite, the suite she'd fled from on New Year's Day, so certain that her husband was having an affair and that their marriage was over.

What else had she been wrong about?

No sooner had he followed her into the room than he spun her around, forcing her back against the door and trapping her with his arms. Before she had a second to protest, his mouth fell on hers, pressing her lips apart, forcing his way inside. It was a harsh, punishing kiss that made no allowances, taking no prisoners as he ravaged her mouth with untempered passion.

It wasn't a kiss that required anything of her. It was a kiss that took, a kiss that spoke to her of anger and frustration and near loss.

At length he raised his head, his breathing ragged and his chest heaving. He put one hand in her hair, screwing a handful into a fist.

'What made you run away?'

She winced a little as her hair pulled taut and touched a tongue to her upper lip. It felt swollen and plump, still tingling from the demanding pressure of his mouth. He relaxed his grip, working his fingers through her hair.

'Why did you leave?'

Why did she leave? There were so many reasons. Where would she start?

'I thought… New Year's Eve—'

'It was you who phoned?'

She frowned. Nodded. 'Someone answered. I thought it was Emma. I thought…' She squeezed her eyes shut shaking her head.

'You thought I was having an affair.'

'Yes. But instead you'd found my mother. That's why you went to England—to find her?'

'Yes,' he said, his voice husky and low. 'I couldn't tell you before I went. I wasn't sure if it was her, or if she'd want to come back.'

'What made you think she was alive?'

He shrugged and drew the pad of his thumb around the line of her jaw, making her breath hitch with the sudden change in his touch, from angry to tender. 'I wasn't sure, not at first. But something you said on the island, that you thought your mother should have survived, only to be told she'd died, had me wondering. I sought a death certificate, thinking that it might at least give you some sense of closure. There was none. Then I knew that things were not as you'd been told.'

'But how did you find her?'

'I had investigators scour the records. They found evidence she'd left the country but the trail was cold—your mother had changed her name. That's when I paid a visit to your father's solicitor. Eventually I convinced him that he was better off telling me the truth, before I buried him with it. Then he was most helpful.'

'Thank you,' she said, 'though those words don't come near to expressing how it feels to have my mother again. Although…' She hesitated. 'I still don't understand why you did this.'

He breathed deep. 'On the island, that same day you spoke of your parents, for the first time I got some idea of just what I had done by forcing you into this marriage.' His fingers moulded themselves to the contours of her neck. 'And I thought that maybe I could find a way to ease some of your pain, to discover what really happened.'

She swallowed, thinking back to that day on the beach, his sudden mood swing finally making sense. He'd set out to find her mother and she'd rewarded him by thinking the worst.

'I'm sorry I thought you were with Emma,' she whispered. 'I'm sorry I doubted you, but after what happened on our wedding night—'

'Hold on,' he said, pulling back. 'Emma *was* there,

for five minutes, but I didn't invite her. When your mother came to the door Emma answered the phone, no doubt hoping it was you. But what did you mean about our wedding night?'

She stared up at him, perplexed. *As if he didn't know.*

'Our wedding night, when you left. Someone saw you getting into a taxi with Emma.'

'*Merdi.*' He spun around, striding halfway across the room. 'And you think I would spend my wedding night, when I had just married you, with another woman?'

'Well, didn't you? You certainly didn't spend it with me.' She peeled herself away from the door and headed for the opposite side of the room.

'I didn't spend it with you because you made it quite clear you didn't want me anywhere near you that night.'

'So you spent it with Emma instead. You were seen getting into a taxi together after all.'

'And was I also seen returning in another taxi, alone, ten minutes later?' He looked sideways at her. 'No?'

She looked at him. Was he telling the truth? 'But you took off to America the very next day. You expect me to believe that had nothing to do with Emma?'

He threw his hands into the air. 'What is this preoccupation of yours with Emma? She is nothing to me.'

'You didn't spend our wedding night with her?'

'I came back and went to the office,' he hissed. 'I

spent my night tangling with spreadsheets, not lying between them.' He moved closer. 'What kind of man do you think I am?'

She dropped her eyes quickly. Too quickly. He closed the distance between them and took her by the shoulders, giving her a solid shake.

'You actually believe I could do that?'

'No! Well—it's just—your reputation…'

'My…reputation?' he said, his mouth curving.

'You had lots of girlfriends before I came along. And you just wanted a family, a baby from me. I wanted to believe I was special to you, but once I was pregnant, I thought…'

He lifted her chin, stroked her bottom lip with the pad of his thumb. 'You feared I was going to treat you like your own mother had been treated. Abandoned while I had my pick of women. Is that it?'

Her eyes misted and she let her head drop, a silent affirmation.

He pulled her in tight to his chest, so tight she could feel the strong beat of his heart, feel the warmth from his body leaching into hers.

'Haven't you learned anything about me these past few months?' He kissed the top of her head.

'I have. I think maybe I underestimated you. Big time. You weren't even supposed to know about Pearl's Place. When did you find out?'

'You think I would go into any business deal without knowing everything?'

She looked up at him, realising how naïve she'd been, having known what a superb businessman he was and yet still thinking she could keep anything secret from him.

'And I liked what I found,' he continued. 'Someone who had all the money that she needed but who chose to share it with those in trouble. Someone who, when her whole business and life were threatened with financial disaster, found a way, indeed, sought out her own way, to continue her business and also her good works.'

His lips met hers, ever so briefly. 'When are you going to understand? I married you. I sleep with you. For some strange reason I even think I love you.'

'No,' she said, her head bolting away, disbelieving. 'You don't love me. You can't.' She pulled out of his embrace and hugged her arms to her chest.

'How do you know what I'm capable of?'

'But you didn't marry me because of love. You married me because you wanted one hundred per cent of Clemengers and I wouldn't give it to you. There was no other reason.'

'Well,' he shrugged, his head to one side, 'maybe just one.'

She looked at him, eyes narrowed, curious but wary. 'What?'

'You intrigued me, you were beautiful, so confident at times and yet so innocent with it. I wanted you from the very first time you burst into my office. When you insisted my share of Clemengers could not be a controlling interest, I had to find a sweetener for the deal. You were that sweetener.'

He moved closer. 'I didn't realise just how sweet until I got you alone, on the island.' He took hold of her arms and unwrapped them from her chest, feeling her doubt and wanting to banish it for ever.

'Do you realise how sexy it is to discover your wife is a virgin? Do you realise how sexy it is to learn no man has had your wife, has felt her curves or dipped his tongue to all her secret places?'

He lowered his head, tracing the tip of his tongue into the curve above her shoulder blade. She gasped, her swift intake of air matched by the expansion of her chest, pushing her breasts out towards him. He cupped one in his hand, feeling the firm peak pressing against his palm, even through the cotton of her T-shirt, the lace of her bra.

'And yet she responds to your every move like a tigress unleashed. How could I not fall in love with such a woman when she is everything that a man could ask for?'

She swayed in his arms, losing all sense of space and time.

He loved her. Truly loved her. Never had she imagined such a thing was possible from a marriage orchestrated entirely by contract. It had been enough to wish that they might possibly survive the years in civility.

'And that's why I would never be unfaithful to you. Never. You need to understand that.'

'I think I do,' she said, her head buzzing, her heart beating madly. 'I wanted to believe that all along. I wanted to but I was too scared to believe it could be true.'

'Oh,' he said, 'it's true.'

'Do I still need to tell you why I ran away?'

His beautiful dark eyes narrowed, his mouth turning up on one side, making a crease in his cheek she moved to run her finger along. 'Because you thought I was with Emma?'

'But did it occur to you why that would matter?'

It was her turn to smile, her turn to wait for his response.

His brow knitted. 'You expected to hate me. I gave you just cause by forcing you into this marriage. And then you suspect I am making love with another. I know I can't expect you to like me, but I can ask that you forgive me for treating you so badly in the first place.'

'But that's not why I ran away.'

'Then why?'

'Because the one thing I was most scared of had happened to me. The one thing I had protected myself against my whole life.'

She reached for his hands, feeling the blood beating within his, echoing her own rapid pulse. 'I fell in love with you, Domenic, and I fell hard. I didn't want to. I put all sorts of barriers and walls up, but you broke through them all.

'Even when I told myself that you would never commit to any one woman, I wanted to believe you might one day commit to me.

'That's why I ran away. Because I love you and because I was afraid that you would never love me back, and I could never, ever live with that.'

He reached his arms around her, pulling her curves in tight against him, so she could feel every muscle and ridge in his body pressed hard against hers and know that he was hers, for now and for always.

'Mrs Silvagni,' he said, his lips closing upon hers. 'As long as I'm around, you'll never have to.' He paused.

'I love you, Opal. There will never be a question of me not loving you back. I will always love you.'

'As I will always love you.'

He kissed her then and she kissed him back, hearts and souls intertwined, knowing that their lives had changed irrevocably this day, that nothing would ever be the same for them and that life in each other's arms would be nothing short of for ever.

'Now,' he said, releasing his hold on her a fraction, 'how about that shower?'

She beamed up at him. 'I thought you'd never ask.'

Mediterranean Brides

**Two billionaires, one Greek, one Spanish—
will they claim their unwilling brides?**

Meet Sandor and Miguel, men who've taken all the prizes
when it comes to looks, power, wealth and arrogance.
Now they want marriage with two beautiful women.
But this time, for the first time, both Mediterranean
billionaires have met their matches and it will take more
than money or cool to tame their unwilling mistresses—
try seduction, passion and possession!

Eleanor Wentworth has always been unloved and
unwanted. Greek tycoon Sandor Christofides has wealth
and acclaim—all he needs is Eleanor as his bride.
But is Ellie just a pawn in the billionaire's game?

BOUGHT:
THE GREEK'S BRIDE
by Lucy Monroe

On sale June 2007.

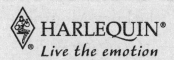

REQUEST YOUR FREE BOOKS!

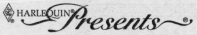 HARLEQUIN *Presents*

PASSION GUARANTEED SEDUCTION

2 FREE NOVELS PLUS 2 FREE GIFTS!

YES! Please send me 2 FREE Harlequin Presents® novels and my 2 FREE gifts. After receiving them, if I don't wish to receive any more books, I can return the shipping statement marked "cancel." If I don't cancel, I will receive 6 brand-new novels every month and be billed just $3.80 per book in the U.S., or $4.47 per book in Canada, plus 25¢ shipping and handling per book and applicable taxes, if any*. That's a savings of close to 15% off the cover price! I understand that accepting the 2 free books and gifts places me under no obligation to buy anything. I can always return a shipment and cancel at any time. Even if I never buy another book from Harlequin, the two free books and gifts are mine to keep forever.

106 HDN EEXK   306 HDN EEXV

Name	(PLEASE PRINT)	
Address		Apt. #
City	State/Prov.	Zip/Postal Code

Signature (if under 18, a parent or guardian must sign)

Mail to the **Harlequin Reader Service®:**
IN U.S.A.: P.O. Box 1867, Buffalo, NY 14240-1867
IN CANADA: P.O. Box 609, Fort Erie, Ontario L2A 5X3

Not valid to current Harlequin Presents subscribers.

Want to try two free books from another line?
Call 1-800-873-8635 or visit www.morefreebooks.com.

* Terms and prices subject to change without notice. NY residents add applicable sales tax. Canadian residents will be charged applicable provincial taxes and GST. This offer is limited to one order per household. All orders subject to approval. Credit or debit balances in a customer's account(s) may be offset by any other outstanding balance owed by or to the customer. Please allow 4 to 6 weeks for delivery.

Your Privacy: Harlequin is committed to protecting your privacy. Our Privacy Policy is available online at www.eHarlequin.com or upon request from the Reader Service. From time to time we make our lists of customers available to reputable firms who may have a product or service of interest to you. If you would prefer we not share your name and address, please check here. ☐

HP07

**He's proud, passionate, primal—
dare she surrender to the sheikh?**

Feel warm winds blowing through your hair
and the hot desert sun on your skin as you are transported
to exotic lands. As the temperature rises, let yourself be
seduced by our sexy, irresistible sheikhs.

Ruthless Sultan Tariq can have anything he wants—
except oil heiress Farrah Tyndall. Now Tariq needs to
marry Farrah to secure a business deal. Having broken
her heart, can he persuade her to love again?

THE SULTAN'S
VIRGIN BRIDE

by Sarah Morgan

On sale June 2007.